"Don't be nice to me right now. I need you to be a detective."

"Counselor, you're scaring me."

"Join the club. The numbers. They're a countdown." She told him about the weekly letters she'd stashed away and the caller who seemed to think she ought to be dead. "Today is day zero. Today is when he planned to attack me. I think he's coming to kill me."

"Did you report it to the police?"

She hugged her arms around her waist. "Would it have done any good? Aren't I the enemy? Someone has been threatening me, and maybe... maybe I wasn't scared enough for him. I'm too stubborn and independent..." Kenna swayed with exhaustion and fell silent.

"Can I be nice to you now?" Keir's voice was deep pitched, calm.

All she could do was nod. He turned her into his arms.

KANSAS CITY COUNTDOWN

USA TODAY Bestselling Author

JULIE MILLER

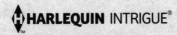

To my fellow Whovians.

You know who you are.

(And please don't ask me to pick a favorite Doctor!)

ISBN-13: 978-0-373-69946-9

Kansas City Countdown

Copyright © 2016 by Julie Miller

Recycling programs for this product may not exist in your area.

Printed in U.S.A.

Julie Miller is an award-winning *USA TODAY* bestselling author of breathtaking romantic suspense—with a National Readers' Choice Award and a Daphne du Maurier Award, among other prizes. She has also earned an *RT Book Reviews* Career Achievement Award. For a complete list of her books, monthly newsletter and more, go to juliemiller.org.

Books by Julie Miller

Harlequin Intrigue

The Precinct: Bachelors in Blue

APB: Baby
Kansas City Countdown

The Precinct: Cold Case

Kansas City Cover-Up
Kansas City Secrets
Kansas City Confessions

The Precinct

Beauty and the Badge
Takedown
KCPD Protector
Crossfire Christmas

The Precinct: Task Force

The Marine Next Door
Kansas City Cowboy
Tactical Advantage
Assumed Identity
Task Force Bride
Yuletide Protector

Visit the Author Profile page at Harlequin.com for more titles.

CAST OF CHARACTERS

Keir Watson—A third-generation cop and the youngest of the Watson brothers, this detective never backs down from a challenge. The last person he expects to stumble out of an alley and into his arms is the attorney who just shredded his latest case.

Kenna Parker—A successful, driven criminal-defense attorney, she has plenty of enemies. When she's brutally assaulted and left with amnesia, she is dismayed by the frightening number of suspects who might want to hurt her. The only man she trusts is the detective who rescued her, Keir Watson.

Helmut Bond—Good ol' Hellie was a friend of Kenna's father, and would like to be an even better friend to her.

Dr. Andrew Colbern—The cosmetic surgeon has been accused of hiring someone to murder his wife.

Devon Colbern—The doctor's aggrieved wife doesn't feel justice has been served. Yet.

Marvin Bennett—Is the Parker estate's gardener about to lose his job? Or his life?

Hudson Kramer—Keir's partner might be a little jealous of his partner's luck with the ladies.

B.J.—Who was Kenna planning to meet the evening she was attacked? And why would she keep that meeting a secret?

Hoodie Guy—When you don't know a name and haven't seen a face, you give the creepy guy who keeps showing up a nickname.

Thomas Watson—Keir's father. Someone has targeted his family. Can the threats against the people he loves be related to the woman his son is protecting?

Seamus Watson—Keir's grandfather. He can't walk by himself and can barely speak. But he knows how to charm a lady.

Prologue

"You're a bad boy, Detective Watson."

Keir Watson laughed at the teasing gibe from Natalie Fensom Parker, the bridesmaid he was escorting down the aisle at his sister's wedding. He adjusted the cherry-red bow tie that matched the vest he wore with his black tuxedo and doffed a salute to Al Junkert as they walked past. Al was an old family friend and KCPD senior officer who'd once partnered with Keir's father, Thomas, before a shattered leg had forced Thomas into early retirement from the department. "No, ma'am. I'm a truth teller. You are absolutely the prettiest pregnant lady here today. The guests can't keep their eyes off you."

Natalie's bouquet of red and white carnations seemed to rest on her swollen belly as she giggled. "Everyone's eyes will be on your sister and Gabe today. Nobody is watching me waddle down the aisle."

"Your husband is."

"Maybe Jim is watching *you*." She beamed a smile to her husband as they walked by. "He and your sister, Olivia, have been partners for some time now. I've got the scoop on all three of you Watson boys. Third generation cops like your father and grandfather before you. He knows your reputation around the precinct offices."

"That I'm a sharp-eyed detective who is as tough as he is resourceful? That I'll make sergeant detective and be running my own task force before I turn thirty-five?"

"No, that you're a flirt." Her fingers squeezed his arm to take the sting out of the accusation. "But Jim assures me you're harmless."

"Natalie, you wound me."

"Well, better me than my husband."

"The warning is duly noted." Keir patted Natalie's hand and grinned. Jim Parker was a lucky man to have this woman love him. His soon-to-be brother-in-law, Gabe Knight, was lucky to have Liv so head over heels for him. And though Keir modestly suspected that there was at least one single woman in the crowded church he could charm into going home with him by the end of the wedding reception, he instead felt a stab of envy that these good people had found their happily-ever-afters. Not that he'd ever admit that little taste of bitterness out loud.

Marriage vows and 2.5 children just weren't in the cards for the youngest Watson brother.

Once he'd wanted what his father and late mother had had until she'd been torn from their lives by her senseless murder by a doped-up thief. He'd seen how devastated his father had been. Keir had felt the grief just as keenly, though as an eleven-year-old he hadn't quite understood why his mother wasn't coming home or why Grandpa Seamus and a new housekeeper/cook were coming to live with them.

Once he'd wanted that goofy smile kind of happiness Natalie and Jim Parker shared. Like them, he'd imagined starting his own family one day. A few years back he'd almost taken the plunge. But patience wasn't always a virtue. He'd waited too long to put his heart on the line. He'd let the high standard of his mother's example of what he wanted in a wife and his ambitious career plans with KCPD get in the way of grasping happiness when the opportunity presented itself.

With the engagement ring he'd hoped to give her buried in his pocket, Keir had waited hours for Sophie Collins to meet him at the restaurant where he'd planned to propose, only to find out the next day that she'd eloped with a friend of his from the police academy—the same man who'd introduced them two years earlier. While he'd been busy studying for his detective's exam and taking extra training courses to be ready for any assignment opportunity, letting the relationship slide to the back burner, the other two had been spending lots of time together. Sophie considered Keir to be the friend, expected him to be happy for her. So he'd kissed her cheek, said all the right words and walked away.

He'd been walking away ever since.

That day, he'd picked his pride up off the floor and closed off his heart to that kind of loss and humiliation ever again. He wasn't averse to enjoying a woman's company, and took pride in being a gentleman and showing a lady a good time—whichever she preferred. But let anything get too serious, too close to feeling like he was giving a woman control over his heart, and Keir moved on. He had plenty of friends, and his career at KCPD was taking off. He'd made detective that first year he was eligible and he'd gotten several plum assignments, including his position now with the major case squad.

What more could a man need to have a successful life?

Right. Family. As Keir neared the front of the church, he reached out and squeezed his hand over the shoulder of his grandpa, Seamus Watson. The eighty-year-old retired KCPD desk sergeant laid his bony fingers over Keir's and smiled, and Keir knew he had all the love a man could need with this close, supportive family. He caught the smile of the plump, silver-haired woman sitting behind Seamus and winked. Grinning at the blush that colored her cheeks, Keir blew a kiss to Millie Leighter, the woman who'd raised him and his brothers and sister after their mother's death. More aunt or grandmother than housekeeper and cook, Millie was family, too.

Yeah. Keir Watson had enough for his life to be a success. The past was what it was. He was moving on.

He released Natalie as they'd rehearsed the night before and joined his older brothers—Duff, the detective, and Niall, an autopsy doctor at the KCPD Crime Lab—on the top step of the altar. A grin curved his lips as he saw Niall adjusting the dark frames of his glasses and nailing him with a piercing glare.

"Natalie is married to Liv's partner, you know," Niall whispered.

"Relax, Charm School Dropout." Keir clapped his tallest brother on the shoulder of his matching black tuxedo and moved in behind him. "Young or old, married or not—it never hurts to be friendly."

Olivia must have given Niall a directive about keeping his brothers in line, because the bespectacled medical examiner now turned his attention to Keir's oldest brother, Duff. "Seriously? Are you packing today?"

Duff's massive shoulders shifted as he turned to whisper a response. "Hey. You wear your glasses every day, Poindexter. I wear my gun."

"I wasn't aware that you knew what the term *Poindexter* meant."

"I'm smarter than I look," was Duff's terse response.

Keir couldn't let that straight line go without saying something. "He'd have to be."

Duff turned his square jaw toward Keir. "So help me, baby brother, if you give me any grief today, I will lay you out flat."

He probably could. If Niall was the brains of the family, Duff was definitely the brawn. But Keir had vowed from a tender age to never go down without a fight—or at least without a smart-aleck protest or two.

But before he could utter the barb on the tip of his tongue, Niall was shushing them. "Zip it. Both of you. You, mind your manners." Keir put up a hand, acquiescing to the terse command, while Niall got on Duff's case, too. "And you stop fidgeting like a little kid."

Then the organ music coming from the wall of pipes in the church's balcony changed and all three brothers turned their attention to the archway at the back of the church. Everyone in the congregation stood and watched Olivia Mary Watson and their father, Thomas, pause a moment before heading down the long aisle together.

Keir's breath caught in his chest as he watched his sister and father approach. They both carried themselves proudly and walked with a purpose, despite Thomas Watson's limping gait. Good grief! When had his tomboy little sister grown up to be such a beautiful woman? She was a detective like him, for Pete's sake, and usually sported jeans and leather jackets. But today, sparkles and lace clung to curves sisters weren't supposed to have. The veil of Irish lace that sat on her dark hair framed blue eyes like his own, and took Keir back several years to the pictures he remembered seeing of their mother and father's wedding day.

"Dude." Duff was about to wax poetic, giving voice to a sentiment similar to what Keir was feeling. "Gabe, you are one lucky son of a—"

"Duff." Leave it to Niall to maintain a necessary sense of decorum.

"You'd better treat her right." Duff whispered a warning to the groom.

"We've already had this conversation, Duff," Niall pointed out. "I'm convinced he loves her."

Gabe never took his eyes off Olivia as he leaned back toward his soon-to-be brothers-in-law. "He does."

This conversation was pointless to Keir's way of thinking. "Anyway, Liv's made her choice. You think any one of us could change her mind? I'd be scared to try."

The minister hushed the lot of them as father and bride approached.

"Ah, hell." Duff was tearing up. "This is not happening to me."

Keir blinked rapidly. If he wasn't careful, he might

embarrass himself and do the same thing. "She looks the way I remember Mom."

Niall slipped Duff a handkerchief while Olivia shared a tight hug with their father. Keir gave her a thumbs-up when she smiled at the three of them, then turned his attention to the exchanging of vows and rings.

By the end of the ceremony, Keir was feeling that sting of envy again, a hollowness that seemed to fill the area of his chest right around his heart.

"You may now kiss the bride."

But he'd made his choices. He was genuinely happy for his sister. While Liv's new husband planted an embarrassingly thorough kiss on her lips, the guests applauded and Keir whistled a cheer between his teeth. Then the recessional started and the happy couple proceeded down the aisle to acknowledge all the family, friends and coworkers gathered here. Duff followed with the matron of honor. Niall took the arm of his bridesmaid and Keir extended his arm to walk Natalie back to her husband and get going to the party to find someone who could make him forget, for a little while, at least, that he wasn't missing a thing by not putting his heart on the line again.

He even danced the first few steps in time with the music until he caught a glimpse of movement up in the balcony. A door opened beside a limestone buttress near the organist. The man who stepped in was dressed in black from head to toe. That was no guest. "What the...?"

By the time Niall shouted, "Gun!" and the recessional ended on an abrupt, dissonant chord, the masked man upstairs had pulled a rifle from beneath his long coat and opened fire down into the church. Keir cursed as he reached for a gun at his waist that wasn't there and pulled Natalie to the floor behind the front pew.

Gunfire exploded in the air and chips of wood blasted over their heads and rained down as the shooter emptied his rifle into the congregation.

Keir was calling Dispatch for a SWAT unit when he heard Duff yell for everybody to get down and heard more chatter among the many police officers in the crowd—getting guests to safety, pinpointing the shooter's location, making plans to go after the man. A matter of seconds passed as the shooter emptied his clip. The momentary pause meant he was reloading, pulling another gun or running. Now was the time to move.

"Stay put," Keir warned Natalie, turning on the camera on his phone. He raised the device over the pew, snapping pictures and getting a position on the shooter before crawling into the aisle. "Damn." New gun. Keir scrambled toward his father, grandfather and Millie as the man pulled a semiautomatic pistol from his belt and sprayed the church with more bullets. A chunk of marble spit off the floor and smacked into Keir's leg.

What the hell was the guy aiming at? Was he blind? Going for chaos over accuracy? The minister at the front of the church was crouched behind the pulpit, and though there were children crying and shouts of panic, Keir couldn't see signs that anyone was hurt or administering first aid. He didn't intend to give the guy the opportunity to improve his aim. He might only have milliseconds to reach his family before the shooter turned his gun back in this direction. "Dad? Grandpa? Millie?"

Keir reached his family, ducking between the seats as a bullet shredded the lacy bow decorating the pew beside him. He pushed Millie to the floor and reached over the seat to help the others. Seamus's cane clattered to the floor.

"Grandpa!" Keir felt the spatter of warm blood hit his cheek a split second before the old man crumpled against Thomas. "Ah, hell."

Seamus Watson had been hit.

Keir shrugged out of his jacket and tossed it on the marble floor beneath his grandfather as his father lowered him to the floor. The rage of bullets fell silent and he spared a glance up at the door closing in the balcony as the shooter escaped, silently swearing to track down the bastard. He pulled a shocked, weeping Millie into his chest and turned her away from the blood pooling on the floor as his brother Niall worked on their grandfather's wound.

Keir had already made one call to Dispatch, but he dialed the number a second time and repeated the call for help, making sure an ambulance was en route. "I need a bus. Now. Officer down. I repeat— officer down."

Chapter One

May

Keir dropped the shot of whiskey into his mug of beer and picked it up before the drink foamed over. "Here's to the Terminator."

His partner, Hudson Kramer, dressed in work boots and blue jeans, lowered his bottle of beer to the bar top. "Please tell me that's sarcasm."

"Loud and bitter, my friend." The Shamrock Bar tonight was loud with Irish music, conversation, laughter, the periodic clinks of glassware and the sharp smacks of pool balls caroming off each other. The frenetic, celebratory energy was typical for a Friday night where several denizens from the KCPD and surrounding downtown neighborhood liked to hang out. They'd survived another week of long hours and hard work that could be, at turns, tedious and dangerous. Some of his fellow cops here had broken cases wide-open this week or arrested criminals or even just kept a drunk driver off the streets, where he could be a threat to the citizens they'd all sworn to serve and protect.

But Keir and Hud, yin and yang in both style and background, yet as close as Keir was to his own brothers, had nothing to celebrate. Keir was feeling the need to either get drunk or get laid to ease the tension coiling inside him.

Sure, some of it had to do with his frustration over the slow-moving investigation into the shooting at the church where his grandfather had nearly died— an investigation that he and his two older brothers weren't allowed to be a part of in any official capacity. Not that departmental restrictions were going to stop Keir and his brothers from pursuing answers for themselves. A masked shooter who threatened a building full of cops on a happy occasion and then disappeared into thin air made every officer in the department an investigator until the perp who'd targeted Keir's family could be identified and caught.

No, tonight's extra-special foray into moody sarcasm all had to do with a leggy, ash-blond defense attorney who'd made mincemeat out of the attempted murder-for-hire investigation he and Hud had turned over to the DA's office on Monday. It had taken Kenna Parker only five days of motions and court appearances to punch holes in their airtight case. The hoity-toity plastic surgeon who'd talked to Keir in an undercover op about hiring him to kill his estranged wife before she could divorce him and cost him a fortune in alimony had gotten off with little more than a slap on the wrist.

Yes, the guy was now under an ethics investigation by the state medical board—a sidebar that could cost him his license or, at the very least, put a dent in his lucrative medical practice. But that wasn't the same as a judge acknowledging that Detective Keir Watson had done his job right. Kenna "the Terminator" Parker hadn't even really cleared Dr. Andrew Colbern of conspiracy to commit murder—she'd just raised enough doubts about Keir's competence and a few seconds of static on the recording he'd made of the conversation that Colbern was walking.

"Did you see how she booked it out of the courtroom right after the judge announced his ruling?" Hud punctuated his condemning tone with a long swallow of his beer. "That's just rubbing her victory in our faces."

Keir eyed the foamy amber liquid in his mug. "She probably went off to pop open a magnum of champagne at our expense."

Hud turned the brown bottle in his hand, then grinned. "Well, then let's just hope she's drinkin' it alone, my friend."

"You got that right." Keir clinked his mug against Hud's bottle, but he couldn't match his partner's good humor.

They'd failed to prove Colbern's guilt beyond a

reasonable doubt, according to the Terminator. Interesting what kind of justice a lot of money and a killer law firm could buy.

Well, reputation meant everything to him, too. Keir Watson didn't botch cases. When he investigated a crime, he got answers. No matter how long it took, he got the job done.

"I swear that woman is going to make me a better cop," Keir vowed, remembering the smug smile on her copper-tinted lips as she'd packed up her briefcase and passed him on her way out of the courtroom. "Next time she shows up in court, she won't be able to raise the issue of entrapment and question technicalities or make her client look more like the victim than the woman he tried to have killed. The next time I'm testifying against one of her clients, I'll make her look like the idiot."

Hud raised his bottle again. "Then, to the downfall of the Terminator."

"Amen." Keir swallowed a healthy portion of the beer and whiskey, savoring the heat seeping down his gullet. Half a drink later, Keir still couldn't erase the tension in him and felt himself turning inward, replaying each step of the case he'd put together, and each trick Kenna Parker had used to pull it apart.

He loosened his tie and unbuttoned his collar, only half listening to Hud regale him with a story about his first encounter with an attorney as a teenager, protesting a ticket in his small-town traffic court.

Something about the lawyer being the judge's second cousin's daughter's boyfriend, and the judge declaring a conflict of interest and dismissing the speeding ticket because the guy was family, and there wasn't anyone else in town who wasn't related who could represent him. Hardly a problem someone with Kenna Parker's legal eagle pedigree would ever have to face.

Sitting here tonight, fuming over the case that had gotten tossed, Keir knew he wasn't very good company. Hud, on the other hand, could blow off the tension once he was away from the job in ways that Keir wasn't able to. Maybe he'd better cut his partner loose to play a game of pool or share a drink with one of the local ladies who had a thing for cops. Keir downed the last of his beer and Bushmill's and pushed the mug away, intent on heading home where he could stew in silence—or more likely, pull out his case file against Andrew Colbern and reread the transcript of his undercover conversation to figure out exactly where he'd misspoken so he wouldn't make the same mistake again.

He clapped Hud on the shoulder of his plaid flannel shirt and stood. "Hey, buddy, I'm heading home."

Hud threw up his hands and frowned. "You're kiddin' me, right? The night is young and this place is crawlin' with opportunities." His brown eyes swept the bar, indicating the disproportionate number of female to male customers. "I need you to be my wingman."

Chuckling at his partner's humorous determination, Keir tossed a couple of bills onto the bar to pay for their drinks. "Sorry. Guess I'm lousy company tonight."

"Tell me about it. I'm givin' you my best stuff and all I've gotten out of you is a smirk."

Keir conceded the truth with a nod. "It's not your job to make things right when a case goes wrong."

"The hell it isn't." Hud polished off the last of his beer and swiped his knuckles over his mouth to erase the foamy mustache. "You'll still be in a mood when you come back to work on Monday, and I'm the guy who has to look at you all day." He pushed aside the money Keir had put on the bar and set a twenty-dollar bill in its place. "I dare you to stay and have a little fun. I know there's a lady here tonight who can put a full-blown smile on your face and make you forget all about the Terminator. In fact, I'll bet you that last round of drinks that I can score some action and be smiling before you."

"Really?" Hud knew his weakness for refusing to back down from a dare. Keir's older brothers had given him plenty of practice at holding his own growing up. Still, he was about to tell his partner that he'd take that bet on some other night when he wasn't quite so tired or distracted, when the Shamrock's owner, Robbie Nichols, set a beer and shot on the bar in front of him. Keir frowned. "I didn't order this."

The bushy-bearded Irishman nodded toward someone behind Keir's back and winked. "She did. Good luck to you, Detective."

Keir turned to see a sweet little strawberry blonde smiling at him as she wove her way through the maze of tables to reach him. Maybe he should take a lesson from his laid-back partner and blow off a little steam. Suddenly, spending Friday night at home with work wasn't as appealing as it had sounded a minute ago. "Are you responsible for this?" he asked the man staring, openmouthed, beside him.

"I wish." Hud had turned, too, and was shaking his head. "Even on your worst night, the ladies love you. Why don't I have that kind of luck?"

"Because you're half hillbilly. And—" Keir buttoned his collar and adjusted his tie as the young woman approached "—a man in a well-tailored suit is like catnip to the ladies." Keir picked up the drink. "I promise you, my friend—if you're going to bet me, you're going to lose."

Robbie returned, popping the cap off a chilled bottle of beer and setting it in front of Hud. "Not to worry, Detective Kramer. The ladies got you one, too."

"Ladies? As in plural?" Quickly tucking his shirt into his jeans, Hud stood beside Keir, focusing in on the burgundy-haired woman with glasses trailing after her friend. "Game on, catnip boy."

The strawberry blonde reached them before Keir could respond to Hud's challenge. "Hi. I'm Tammy. I hope you're not leaving. My sister and I took a vote and decided you were the cutest guy here."

Cute? Well, now, didn't that make him feel about twice this girl's age and a little less eager to win the bet? Still, from a very young age, his mama had taught him to have manners, so Keir extended his hand. "I'm flattered. Keir Watson. Thank you for the drink."

"Keir? That's an unusual name."

"It's Irish. My mother was born in Ireland."

"Awesome."

The shy redhead at her shoulder looked a few years older and a little less enthusiastic about picking up a guy in a bar. She nudged her friend and glanced at Hud. "Tammy, it's getting late. How long is this going to take?"

Poor Hud. He had his work cut out for him if he wanted to win the bet.

Instead of answering, Tammy beamed a smile at Keir's partner. "This is Gigi. My older sister." Tammy emphasized the age difference, as if the three or four years that must separate them meant big sis was over the hill and that she was the prime catch. *Awkward.* Clearly, Tammy was pawning her sister off on Hud, and had eyes only for Keir. "I'll let Gigi tell you what it's short for."

But Hud wasn't complaining. Once the introductions had been completed, he pulled out the stool Keir had vacated and invited Gigi to sit beside him.

Keir smiled down at the strawberry blonde. Whether her sister was shy about men or genuinely tired, Tammy was determined to hit on him. And Gigi seemed to be sufficiently entertained as Hud launched into his good ol' boy spiel. "All right, then. Shall we?"

He picked up his drinks and escorted Tammy to a private table while she asked if the gun and badge he wore were real. Feeling older by the minute and wishing he'd trusted his gut and headed home, Keir briefly considered if this woman might be underage. But he was certain Robbie and his staff would have carded both women before selling them alcohol. Something about running a bar frequented by cops kept a man from bending the rules.

Still, the momentary rush of proving to Hud that (a) he always had his game on with the ladies, and (b) his partner didn't need to worry about his mood, quickly faded. An hour passed and Keir was beginning to feel as though he was watching out for a friend's kid sister rather than seriously considering extending the evening into something more. True, his thoughts kept straying back to those moments in the courtroom when the judge had chastised his unit for not making sure all their ducks were in a row in their case against Dr. Colbern.

But it seemed Tammy couldn't sustain a conversation beyond flirty come-on lines, the classes she was taking at UMKC and all the adventures at bars she and her sister were having now that she'd turned twenty-one. Tammy was pretty. She was sweet. And he had a feeling she was sincere in her interest in him. But twenty-one was too young for a man in his early thirties, and Keir wisely kept the evening platonic until the cocktail waitress announced last call and he decided to call it a night.

Hud and the less animated Gigi had moved over to the pool tables, where he was teaching her some tricks of the game. A quick text exchange with Keir's partner confirmed that they'd hit it off as friends and that Hud was fine giving the young lady a ride home after they finished their last set. Keir conceded the bet and paid for all their drinks.

Tammy was obviously disappointed that Keir decided to call it a night instead of inviting her out on a date or even asking for her number. He tried to soften the blow to her ego. "It's been a long week for me and I'm tired. Plus, if you've got an exam Monday, you'd better try to get a little sleep so you can study this weekend." He stood and took her hand. "Come on. I'll walk you to your car."

He traded a salute with Hud and led Tammy through the dwindling crowd outside the front door.

The days had been warming up with the advent of spring, but the hour was late and there was a chill in the air that elicited an audible shiver from the young woman beside him. Whether her reaction was legit or one last attempt to stir his interest in her, Keir shrugged out of his suit jacket and draped it around her shoulders. "Which way?"

There might be a dozen or more cops inside the bar, but the downtown streets of Kansas City—even in neighborhoods that were being reclaimed like this one—were no place for a woman to be walking alone at night. She pointed past the neon shamrock in the bar's window to the curb on the next block. Making a brief scan of the street and sidewalks, Keir dropped his hand to the small of Tammy's back and headed past the bar's parking lot, the valet stand for a nearby restaurant, past a north-south alley and the sports bar beyond it, then across the intersection to reach her car.

"I'll wait until you get in and get it started," he said, taking back his jacket and slipping into it.

"You're a nice guy, Detective Watson." Tammy latched on to the lapels of his coat and stretched up on tiptoe as he straightened the collar. "Are you sure I can't change your mind about coming home with me? It looks like Gigi and your friend will be a while."

He pried her hands loose and leaned down to kiss her forehead. "Good night, Tammy." He grinned when she slipped a piece of paper into his pocket, suspecting it was the phone number he hadn't asked for. He closed the door behind her once she'd started the engine, and stepped back onto the curb. "Be safe."

Waving as she drove away, Keir loosened his tie and collar again. Time to call it a night. He hadn't gotten drunk. He hadn't gotten laid. And he sure as hell hadn't figured out any answers to the unresolved cases weighing on his mind. Deciding that the night wasn't going to get any better, and his day couldn't get any worse, he turned and strode back toward the parking lot behind the Shamrock where he'd parked his own car.

He nodded to the trio of college-aged men bemoaning a call in the baseball game they'd been watching inside as they exited the sports bar. Then he stepped around the group of suits and dresses waiting for their ride outside the South American restaurant, shrugging at their fancy outfits in this workingman's neighborhood. Keir's attention shifted to a man standing on the sidewalk across the street. Hanging back in the shadows, wearing a dark hoodie, his shoulders hunched over with his hands buried in the pockets of his baggy jeans, the man's face was unreadable. But his focus was unmistakable. There was something about the restaurant, something about the people walking down the street as the bars and restaurants let out, something or someone on this side of the street he was watching so intently that the hood over his head never even moved.

And that's why you walk a lady to her car.

His suspicions pinging with an alert, Keir slowed his pace and stopped, discreetly pulling his phone from his pocket and snapping a picture while pretending to text. He doubted he'd get a clear shot, but he could at least record a location and vague description. But Hoodie Guy saw that he'd been noticed, and quickly spun away and shuffled on down the street.

"That's right, buddy, I'm a cop." Keir watched the man until he turned at the next intersection and disappeared around the corner of a closed-up building. "You're not causing any trouble tonight."

Detouring for a moment, Keir retraced his steps, wondering if there was anything in particular Hoodie Guy had been watching. Maybe he'd been waiting for someone to separate from the pack—someone to mug for drug money or mooch a drink from. Maybe he'd been watching an old girlfriend on a date with someone new. And maybe the guy just had a creepy sense of fashion and poor timing when it came to choosing where he wanted to loiter. There was no way for Keir to get answers unless he wanted to chase the guy down. And, technically, the guy hadn't done anything to warrant such a response.

Satisfied for the moment that the street was safe, Keir turned around and resumed the walk to his car. Keeping one eye on the cars and empty spaces and drivers and pedestrians to see if Hoodie Guy reappeared, he pulled up his messages. Maybe he'd find a victorious text from Hud or news from his family about Seamus Watson's shooting or his health as his eighty-year-old grandfather recovered from the brain injury that had left him relearning how to speak and use the left side of his body. Nothing. Not even an update from the detectives working the investigation.

Keir scrolled through the case notes he sent himself as texts on his phone as he stepped over the cable marking off a neighborhood parking area and cut through the public space to reach the Shamrock's parking lot. He stepped over the cable at the back end of the lot, ignored the retching sounds of a drunk in the alley he passed and climbed a couple of steps over a short concrete wall to reach the lot where his Dodge Charger was parked.

He was considering sending a text to Hud about their failed pickup bet when he heard the scrabble of footsteps and a slurred, feminine voice from the alley behind him.

"One. One. One is the wrong number."

Keir swung around at the garbled words, leaving the text half-finished and pulling back his jacket to rest his hand on his holstered weapon.

A tall, slender woman stumbled to the edge of the alley. "Three… Two… One isn't right."

"Ma'am?" She wasn't drunk and she wasn't a threat. She was hurt. Seriously hurt, judging by the blood on her face and clothes.

She tried to raise her head, but she groaned and

braced her hand against the brick wall as she swayed. "Please. Help me."

Keir leaped over the concrete barrier, taking in several details as he ran to assist the injured woman. Dark silvery blond hair bounced against her chin and clung to the bloody hash marks on one side of her face. The skirt of her fancy tan suit was ripped along one seam and there were dirty smudges on both sleeves of her jacket. She wore one ridiculously sexy leather pump on her right foot, and nothing but a torn silky stocking over the scraped-up knee and toes on her left foot.

"Ma'am, are you all right?" Keir slipped his arm behind her waist, taking her weight and guiding her to the concrete wall. Hoodie Guy's curiosity about something Keir had missed was screaming at him now. Damn it. He should have followed up on his suspicions and stopped the guy for questioning. He helped the lady sit on the edge of the wall, wondering if Hoodie Guy was responsible for this. "What happened?"

"I woke up. I got sick. Everything…spinning."

"Are you alone? Is anyone else hurt?"

She opened her mouth to answer, turned her chin toward the alley, then looked away. "I don't remember."

"Okay." Clearly, she was a little disoriented. "Stay put. I'll be right back."

Once he was certain she wasn't going to collapse

on him, Keir pulled his weapon and darted back into the alley, making a cursory sweep of the trash bins and power poles. He startled a rat from its hiding place. But there was no one else in the alley. No signs of a struggle. Not even the missing shoe. This was a dump site. Whatever had happened to her hadn't happened here.

Maybe Hoodie Guy hadn't attacked her, after all. He'd moved away on foot, and it would be impossible to transport an injured woman through this maze of back alleys without a vehicle or someone noticing the two of them together.

Holstering his Glock, Keir jogged back out of the alley to find her on her feet, limping over to meet him. So much for staying put. "Is anyone else hurt?"

Keir caught her by the elbows and turned her back toward the wall and the nearest lamp in the middle of the lot. "Just you. I thought I told you to wait for me."

"I don't know where I…" she muttered beside him. "I don't know how long I was there." She flattened her hand over her stomach and bent forward, as if she was going to be ill. "I don't feel so good."

"Ma'am?" He stopped her beneath the light and waited for her to nod that she could stand straight again before brushing the angled line of bangs off her forehead. Keir swore under his breath as he tilted her face to the yellowish light. He knew this woman. "Kenna Parker? What the hell are you doing—"

"Who are you?" She squinted against the light

shining in her eyes and backed away from him, fear making her skin pale.

He raised a placating hand to stop her wobbly retreat and pulled his badge from his belt. "I'm Detective Keir Watson, KCPD. Ms. Parker, how badly are you hurt? Can you tell me what happened?"

She shook her head. But the motion made her dizzy and she grabbed the sides of her head and tumbled.

"Watch out." Keir caught her before she hit the ground and scooped her up into his arms. Her cheek fell against his shoulder and she curled into him without a protest as he stepped over the short wall and carried her to his car. "What does *one* mean?" he asked. Maybe her attacker had been wearing a jersey with a number on it, or she'd seen part of a license plate. "Why is it the wrong number?"

"What?" Her fingers curled into the lapel of his jacket. "I don't understand."

"You kept saying… Never mind." Once he got the passenger door open, he set her feet on the pavement and helped her onto the edge of the seat before pulling the first-aid kit out of the glove compartment. "You were mugged. Assaulted. I can't tell how badly yet. Can you tell me who did this to you? Do you know how you got into that alley? I don't think the attack happened there."

He dabbed at the cuts on her face, tried to assess how well her eyes were tracking the movement of his hands as he knelt in front of her. Besides their sensitivity to the light, her pupils were dilated, both signs that she had a concussion. "I should have a purse. Or a briefcase or something. Where are my things? I always carry…" Her voice trailed away and the thought escaped her.

"I didn't see anything like that in the alley. Is *one* part of a phone number? If you need to call someone, you can borrow my phone."

"Who do I need to call?"

He didn't think she was married. There was no ring, nor any sign that she'd ever worn one, on her left hand. "A boyfriend? Any friend? Your doctor? Someone you work with?"

She touched her finger to the drops of blood staining the knobby silk of her jacket and blouse, as if discovering the spots distracted her from the conversation.

Stay with me, lady. Keir slipped two fingers beneath her chin and tilted her face back to his. "Do you want me to call them for you?"

"I can't think of names right now." Her fingertips tickled the back of his wrist as they danced against the skin there. "Aren't you my boyfriend? Isn't that why you're here?"

"No, ma'am." He carefully plucked a stray lock of hair from the wound on her cheek and tucked it behind her ear. "Detective Watson, remember? I showed you my badge."

Instead of answering, she raised her fingers to touch the seeping gash. But Keir ripped open a gauze pad and batted her hand away to stanch the wound. This was more than a mugging or purse snatch. These cuts were fine and deep, made by something with a short, sharp blade. She was damn lucky she still had her eye. Carving up half her face like this indicated a lot of rage, and something very personal. The senseless brutality of this attack wasn't something he'd wish even on the woman who'd humiliated him in court. "Here. Can you hold that there while I check the rest of your injuries?"

"It hurts." Her shaking fingers brushed against his as she reached up to apply pressure against the cut. Her eyes were pale gray, almost like starlight, in the dim illumination of the car's overhead light. But though her voice sounded far less steady and sure than it had in the courtroom that afternoon, she was determined to hold his gaze. "My thoughts aren't very clear, Detective. I can't seem to concentrate. I don't think that's like me."

"It's not."

"So you do know me."

"Yes, ma'am." Keir gently tunneled his fingers into the straight, silky curtain of her chin-length hair, probing her scalp until he found the goose egg and oozy warmth of blood at the base of her skull. She winced and he quickly pulled away to open an emergency ice pack and crush the chemicals together between his hands to activate its frosty chill. He placed the ice pack over the knot on her scalp and tried to estimate if he had enough gauze or something else to anchor it into place. He sought out her starlit eyes again. "Looks like you suffered a pretty good blow to the head. Tell me what you *can* remember."

Although concentrating on the answer seemed to cause her pain, she bravely came up with an answer. "I was going to a meeting. Dinner. A dinner meeting."

Dinner would have been hours ago. "Who was your meeting with?"

"I don't know."

"Where did you eat? Were you walking to your car? Do you remember where you parked? Did a chauffeur or taxi pick you up?"

"I don't know." Seeming to grow more agitated, she pulled the gauze pad from her face and saw the scarlet stain on it. "Is all this blood mine?"

"I need to get you to an ER." She leaned over against the seat, closing her eyes as he placed a call to Dispatch and gave his name, location and badge number. "I need an ambulance…" He dropped the phone into her lap and cupped his palm over the uninjured side of her face. "No, no. Don't close your eyes. Ms. Parker? Kenna? Kenna, open your eyes."

Her silvery eyes popped open. "Stop saying that."

Now, *that* tone sounded like the Terminator. "Are

you kidding me? You're going to the hospital if I have to drive you myself."

"What's happened to me? I don't understand."

"Ah, hell." He swung her legs into the car and buckled her in. "That's it. We'll make sense of this later." He snatched up the phone and relayed the necessary information to complete the call before shrugging out of his jacket and draping it over her like a blanket. "We're going to the hospital, Kenna."

She grabbed the front of his shirt as he leaned over her, pulling her injured face close to his. "Why do you keep calling me that?"

"Fine," he snapped. "You're Ms. Parker. Don't suppose I can get away with calling you the Terminator to your face."

Her pale lips trembled. "Why would you do that?"

He was a sorry SOB for losing his temper for even one moment with this woman. She was probably five or six years older than Keir, and had been his enemy in the courtroom. He had less in common with her than that Tammy Too-Young from the bar. But he couldn't look at the tragedy that marred her beautiful face or the fear that darted in the corner of her eyes and not feel something. He covered her hands where she still held on to him and eased her back into the seat. "I'm sorry. I don't mean to be a jackass. But you're the last person I expected to be helping tonight."

"You don't like me, do you?" She gave him a

graceful out for that question by asking another. "You know who I am?"

"Yes, ma'am. Kenna Parker. You're a criminal defense attorney."

Her fingertips dug into the muscle beneath the cotton of his shirt, holding on when he would have pulled away. "How do you know? You said you couldn't find my purse."

She wanted to argue with him? *Patience, Watson. The woman is scared.* "You shredded a case of mine in court this afternoon. But I'm a cop before anything else. Now something terrible has happened to you tonight. I don't know what exactly, but I'm going to help you."

Her posture sagged, although her grip on him barely eased. He couldn't tell if she was frightened or angry or some combination of both.

"Detective Watson. I don't remember what happened to me tonight, much less this afternoon. I don't know how I got into that alley. I don't know why someone wanted to hurt me like this.

"I don't even remember my name."

Chapter Two

Kenna Parker.

Shivering in an immodest gown in the sterile hospital air, she silently worked the name around her tongue and wondered if she was truly remembering her name or if she'd simply heard it said to her so many times over the past few hours that she was now accepting it as fact.

Kenna.

She was Kenna Parker. She'd been named after her late father, Kenneth. She was an only child, a surprise gift to older parents who'd never expected to have children at all. No one had told her that tonight—or make that the early hours of Saturday morning. Kenna breathed a cautious sigh of relief. She *was* remembering. Some of her life, at least— like the growing-up parts that did her no good answering questions from the clerk at the reception desk or the admitting nurse or the criminologist who'd scraped beneath her fingernails and taken pictures of her injuries before the attending physician went to work.

She couldn't remember whether or not she was in a relationship. She couldn't remember where she'd eaten dinner or even if she had eaten. And hard as she tried, she had absolutely no memory of being brutalized and left for dead, no image of her attacker haunting her thoughts. She had no memory of who hated her or something she represented or had done so much that splitting her head open and taking a sharp blade to the left side of her face seemed justifiable. The nicks on her hands, and the scrapes on her knee and foot, indicated she'd put up a fight. Surely she'd eventually remember a face or mask or height or voice or something if she'd done that kind of battle with her assailant.

But there was a black void in place of where any memory of the assault should be. Bits and pieces of her life before whatever had happened to her tonight were coming together like an old film reel being spliced together. Yet Kenna was afraid some parts of the movie would never be recovered. Even the last few hours after the assault were filled with holes. According to the doctor, scrambled brains were a side effect of the head trauma she'd received. Plus, he'd said that the amnesia could be psychological, as well—that whatever she'd been through had been so awful that her mind might be protecting her from the shock of remembering.

That didn't seem right, though. She wasn't sure why, but Kenna got the feeling from her defensive injuries, and her inability to relax until she figured out at least some part of what had happened to her, that she had a strong will to survive—that Kenneth Parker or someone in her past had taught her to think and fight, not surrender to a weakness like hysterical amnesia.

A glimpse of something sharp and silver glinted in the corner of her eye and Kenna shrieked. "Stop it!" Throwing up her hands, she snatched the man's wrist to stop the sharp object coming at her face.

"Nurse."

"Yes, Doctor." Small hands tugged at her shoulder and Kenna twisted away. "Easy, Ms. Parker. We're trying to help you."

"Get away from me!" Kenna evaded the hands and shoved the weapon away, fighting to sit up.

"Kenna." A firmer hand clasped her shoulder, refusing to be shrugged off. "You're safe. I've got your back."

Kenna froze at the deeply articulate male voice. She tilted her gaze to the dark-haired man with the badge and gun on his belt. Blue eyes. She knew those blue eyes. He was Detective…? The name that went with the piercing gaze escaped her for the moment. Still, she appreciated the clip of authority in his tone. If he said so, she believed he would keep her safe.

"The last thing we need is for her to panic. Isn't that right, Doc?"

The other man chuckled beside her. "It's never a good thing in the ER."

Kenna turned to the gentler voice and looked into the black man's warm brown eyes.

"That's where you are now. St. Luke's Hospital emergency room. You have a concussion, several abrasions and some deep cuts I'm in the process of treating now that I know what medications I can use."

Kenna drew in a deep breath to calm the pulse pounding in her ears and nodded. She dropped her gaze to the plastic ID badge the doctor in the white lab coat wore around his neck. "Dr. McBride." She realized she still had his forearm clenched between her hands and quickly opened her grip. "I'm sorry. I thought you were… That someone was… I don't know what I thought."

"Did you remember something about the attack?" Detective Blue Eyes asked. "Is the syringe significant?"

"There was no evidence of drugs in her preliminary blood work," the doctor offered.

Keir nodded. "But there are some drugs that leave the system quickly."

"That's true. And I estimate these injuries occurred eight to ten hours ago."

"I don't think that's it," Kenna interrupted. "Something was coming at my face. I could see…" A black void filled the space where the memory should be. She shook her head. A syringe? She eyed the object in the doctor's hand and frowned. She couldn't have been cut with a syringe. Her focus narrowed to the tiny hash marks and numbers marking the syringe—*3 ml. 2.5 ml. 2 ml. 1.5…* A door slammed shut in her head and she wanted to scream.

So what did that mean? She tried to recall what it was that had triggered her panicked reaction. But when she closed her eyes to concentrate, she was greeted by the frightening abyss of her amnesia. Kenna quickly opened her eyes to focus on things she could recognize and shook her head. "Sorry. I've still got nothing."

"Not to worry." The detective pulled away, retreating to the doorway where he must have been waiting, out of the doctor's and nurse's way. "We'll figure it out."

"I hope you're right."

He winked. "I'm always right."

His confidence surprised her for a moment before she felt a smile softening her bruised, swollen face. His roguish charm distracted her from her fears and gave her back some of her own confidence. "Then we'd better get to it. I'll do my best not to freak out on anyone again."

While the nurse tucked a warm blanket around her, Dr. McBride rolled his stool back to the examination table and pointed to the items on the stainless steel tray beside him as he explained the procedure. She watched him pick up the syringe again, and her chest grew tight. Kenna breathed in deeply to dispel the uneasiness quaking inside her. Maybe she just had a thing about needles. With the nurse's help, she turned onto her side, looking away from the doctor as he went to work. "Go ahead, Doctor."

"I need you to relax. This is the same localized numbing agent I used on your scalp when I stitched that up. You'll feel three little pinches before I'm done."

Kenna nodded her understanding. If she wasn't going to have any useful kind of flashback, why bother trying to understand? Forcing her jumbled thoughts to organize themselves was only aggravating the headache throbbing against her skull. Maybe if she stopped fighting so hard to remember and didn't focus on anything except her present surroundings, the answers would finally come to her.

Dr. McBride seemed blessedly patient with her and competent in his treatment of her wounds. The nurse buzzed around the ER room, setting equipment and medicines on the tray beside the doctor and taking away discarded items. Detective Blue Eyes—no, wait…Keir Watson. His name fell into place and she smiled inside. Finally. A memory that seemed to stick. Detective Watson was either standing guard at the door or waiting to get the full report on her injuries from the doctor. Kenna wasn't sure why the younger man with the take-charge voice would still be here if it wasn't for some official reason. He'd explained more than once that they didn't have a personal connection. Instead, he'd described them as adversaries from work.

It was a shame to have forgotten a compelling face like Keir's. Chiseled bone structure that was perhaps a bit too sharp to be traditionally handsome was softened by a dusting of tobacco-brown beard stubble and a sexy half-grin. Those impossibly blue eyes narrowed with a question when he caught her studying him and she held his gaze until he folded his arms over his chest. The movement drew her attention lower. He'd put his jacket back on and she acknowledged another memory. Seeing how the dark gray wool hugged his shoulders and biceps, Kenna recalled Keir's body heat, and how quickly she'd warmed up with his jacket draped over her in his car. She remembered the faint scents of something oakish and bitter that had clung to the material, too, making her think he'd enjoyed some kind of drink before they'd met.

Or met again.

Or something like that.

Oh, how she hated being at such a disadvantage. Why was Keir her enemy? She'd done something to him. *Shredded a case* of his in court? Just what kind of attorney was she? Not one who worked for the good guys, apparently.

Now, didn't that conjure up all kinds of possibilities as to who might want to hurt her? A client unsatisfied with her representation? The family member of a criminal who'd been sent to prison despite her best efforts? A victim upset because she'd kept someone *out* of prison? Was she trying a controversial case? Had she learned a dangerous secret from one of her clients that someone else was anxious to keep silent?

She didn't think this kind of violence could be random. Maybe the attack had nothing to do with her job. Did she have a jealous ex? A rival at work? It was impossible to evaluate her choices when she couldn't yet recall all the details of her life.

Kenna winced as the needle pricked the skin near her temple and closed her eyes when she felt a second pinch in her hairline. She gritted her teeth when she felt the third shot sting her jaw, and her breathing grew a little more rapid. How much more would she have to endure tonight?

She'd kept herself as calm and focused as she could, under the extreme circumstances. But the emergency room at St. Luke's Hospital in downtown Kansas City was a noisy, overwhelming place, especially for a woman who couldn't answer many of the questions the admitting clerk, attending nurse, emergency room physician or KCPD criminologist who'd left earlier had asked her over the last several hours.

Keir Watson's badge had gotten her through the red tape of checking in, but without an insurance card or a driver's license, the staff couldn't check her medical records. Dr. McBride had refused to give her anything for the pain or even antibiotics until he'd received a fax to back up her shaky assertion that she didn't *think* she was allergic to any medications. She was worn out. There wasn't any part of her that didn't hurt. And the wound to her memory wasn't something that Dr. McBride and his nurse could treat.

Were those tears chafing her eyelids? She wasn't a crier, was she? She'd hate that if she was. Exhaustion and frustration were finally winning the battle against the sheer will to keep it all together.

"Need something to hold on to?"

Kenna's eyes popped open when she felt a warm hand sliding over hers.

Keir Watson's grasp was as sure as the hug of his arms around her body had been when he carried her to his car. It was just as warm and reassuring, too, reminding her she wasn't alone and that someone strong and capable truly did have her back—even if it was only for tonight.

Kenna nodded her thanks and squeezed her fingers around the detective's solid grip. "Thank you. Again."

"Don't worry, Counselor. I'm keeping tabs on what you owe me."

Kenna hoped that his teasing tone was genuine,

because she felt like smiling. Only, the shots had deadened the left side of her face and she couldn't tell if she'd smiled or not. The stiffness from the swelling and the raw ache of the open wounds finally disappeared with a numbing relief.

She squeezed her eyes shut and held on while the doctor worked on the long, deep cuts. He'd already pulled her hair off her forehead and cheek and anchored it off her face with one of those caps she'd seen doctors wear into surgery. Although she couldn't actually see what the doctor was doing, she felt the warmth of the sterile solution he squirted over her cuts and tasted miniscule grit and the coppery tang of her own blood at the corner of her lips before someone wiped it away. She felt the tugs on her skin and heard a couple of concerned sighs and quick orders to the nurse while he glued and sutured and applied tiny butterfly bandages to the wounds.

"I think we're finally done." The doctor rolled his stool away from the table and stood.

The left side of Kenna's face was still numb, her eyelid droopy from the anesthetic, when she finally let go of Keir's hand. He and the nurse helped her sit up and swing her legs over the edge of the table while Dr. McBride rattled off wound-care instructions and washed his hands. He shone a light into her eyes one more time, checking her pupil reaction, before smiling and giving her permission to leave on the proviso that she contact her personal physician Monday morning.

The nurse rolled aside the stainless steel tray piled with bloodied gauze and various tubes of antibiotics and skin glue. After depositing the sharps on the tray in the disposal bin, the nurse handed her several sheets of printed instructions and a package of sterile gauze pads and tape. Meanwhile the doctor reminded her of the symptoms to watch out for that might indicate the injury to her brain was getting worse.

"Thank you, Dr. McBride." Kenna spoke slowly to articulate around the numbness beside her mouth. "I appreciate everything you've done for me."

"You're lucky you can't remember what happened to you, Ms. Parker." He reached out and shook her hand, holding on for a few compassionate seconds. "If the amnesia turns out to be permanent, perhaps that's a good thing. I can't imagine how frightening an attack like that would be. You take care."

After Dr. McBride and the nurse had gone, Kenna tilted her gaze to the detective still standing beside the examination table. "So why don't I feel lucky?"

"Because you don't know who did this to you. And you're afraid he or she might come back to finish the job."

Exactly. "I think I liked you better when you held my hand and didn't say anything."

Keir slid his hands into the pockets of his charcoal

slacks and grinned. "And here I thought you didn't like me at all, Counselor."

Kenna couldn't understand why she wouldn't have found this man charming. True, he seemed to be a few years younger than she was, but not enough to make any awkward difference. She had a feeling his sarcastic sense of humor was very much like her own, and she owed him more than she could repay for rescuing her and standing by her through this whole, tortuous ordeal. She tried to match his smile. "Tell me again why we're supposed to be enemies? I hurt you, didn't I? Hurt someone you care about. Oh, God, I didn't sue you, did I?"

"No. You didn't sue me." He reached over to pluck the surgical cap off her head and let her hair fall around her face. "According to the doctor, I'd better not fill in the blanks. He said that in order for your memory to recover you need to figure out the missing details in your brain for yourself."

That wasn't all Dr. McBride had cautioned her about. "If it comes back at all."

"You want to try again?"

"Try what?"

The detective pulled out his phone to show her a picture of a man wearing a black sweatshirt hoodie and blue jeans. "Do you recognize this man?"

Kenna studied the image for a few seconds. "Did he do this to me?"

"I can't say."

"Because you don't know? Or because you want me to tell you who he is."

Keir's firm mouth eased into a grin. "Can you identify this guy?"

She looked again. Even if she could remember the attack, there was little to identify in the picture. The man stood in the shadows behind a parked car, beneath a harsh circle of light from a street lamp creating shadows that rendered his face a black void that reminded her of the Grim Reaper.

"No. I don't know him." Not even the clothes looked familiar. She tucked the loose hair behind her ears. "What if I never remember what happened to me? How good a detective are you? Can KCPD solve a crime like that? I may not remember clients and faces, but I remember my books and law school and what it takes to make a good case. I can't imagine getting a conviction if the victim herself isn't a reliable witness. Any decent defense attorney would fry me in court."

Keir's eyes darkened to an unreadable midnight blue, and the grin disappeared. She'd struck a nerve there. Something to do with *shredding his case* again, she imagined. A fist squeezed around Kenna's heart. She didn't want whatever had happened between them in the past to ruin this…what? Friendship? Attraction? Maybe she was the only one imagining a connection between them. What if he was just a good cop following through on an investigation and she could have been any citizen he'd taken an oath to protect? Maybe she was more addled in the head than she knew and she couldn't tell the difference between being kind and caring.

Kenna dropped her feet to the floor and stood, reaching for Keir when he turned away. "What did I just say? I reminded you of something. What did I do to you?"

His cell phone vibrated, creating an audible buzz in the silence of the room while she waited for him to answer.

"Keir?"

But an explanation wasn't coming. Keir read the summons on the screen as it buzzed again. "The doc said I couldn't use my phone in here, but I need to take this."

An instinctive response to ask a different question—to get him to open up about something else before she steered the conversation back to what she really wanted to know—kicked in. "Who's calling you before dawn?"

"My partner. I asked him to do a wider search grid around the alley where I found you, see if he could find a primary crime scene or at least where you parked your car. He's searching to find the guy I showed you, too."

"He's a person of interest, isn't he?"

"I spotted him in the general vicinity where I found you. Don't know if he was sizing up a mark, if he was watching the alley to see if anyone noticed you or if he just had nothing better to do on a Friday night. I'd sure like to talk to him." The phone buzzed impatiently, and Keir backed toward the door. "I'll be out in the lobby."

Manipulating the conversation to get to the answer she needed was starting to feel like second nature to her. Had she possessed this stubborn streak before the attack? "Tell me why you called me the Terminator earlier. It didn't sound like a compliment."

"I'll ask up front about getting you some clothes, too, since the CSI took your suit and shoe to the lab."

This conversation wasn't done. Kenna walked right up to him and fingered the lapel of his gray tweed jacket. She rubbed her thumb over the crimson smear staining the nubby material. "You'd better ask about a change of clothes for you, too. You've got blood on your jacket. My blood."

"I'm coming back." The gap—both literal and figurative—widened between them as he pulled the material from her fingers. Then he put the phone to his ear and turned away. "Hey, buddy. What's up?"

Kenna hugged her arms around her weary body and watched the door close behind him. Keir had managed to be supportive and evasive at the same time. "Run, you clever boy."

Clever boy. Where had that phrase come from? While she'd seen glimpses of a boyish charm, there was certainly nothing immature about Keir Watson. Not in his stature, his tone or his demeanor.

"Clever boy," she muttered the words again, mentally chasing the blip of a memory that floated through her head. "It's from a TV show." She watched TV. She had a hobby. "Blue box. British accents." One lightbulb, however dim, finally turned on inside her head. *"Dr. Who."*

She seemed to be in pretty good shape, so she wasn't a full-blown couch potato. Who did she watch it with? Family? Friends? A significant other? Why hadn't whoever she watched that show with come to see her at the hospital? Okay, sure, there was that whole thing with the missing phone and purse and relying on the police to track down where she lived and worked—but wasn't someone missing her? Alarmed that it was five in the morning and she hadn't come home?

Or was someone at home the danger she needed to fear? The person who'd gotten so angry that he or she had tried to kill her? How should she handle this? What was her next step? How was she supposed to know who to trust?

"Take a breath," she warned herself before panic reclaimed her.

Kenna hugged her arms around the thin cotton of her gown and glanced around the room, looking for answers. Looking for someone to talk to. Looking for a friend or sympathetic doctor or polite detective or anyone who could keep this helpless, lonely feeling from seeping in as surely as the air-conditioned chill that dotted her skin with goose bumps.

She had a feeling she wasn't used to relying on others to take care of her. Kenna eyed the soiled remains from treating her injuries that the nurse had wheeled into the corner. She wasn't used to being weak like this, forced to put her trust in people she didn't know. Had she put her trust in the wrong person, making herself a sitting duck who'd had no clue she was about to be attacked?

Fear crawled across her skin as the knowledge she would have to trust someone to help her through this sank in. Where was home? How was she supposed to get there? What was she supposed to do with herself the next morning? And the day after that?

Her gaze drifted over to the ER room's metal door. She'd put her trust in Keir Watson tonight. Not that he'd left her much choice. He'd allowed her a token argument, then had swept her up into his arms, bundled her into his car and driven her here. But she could have asked him to leave the treatment room at any time, and she hadn't. She wanted him with her.

Crazy as it seemed, Kenna knew Keir better than anyone else in her life. Once she'd come to and realized her brain had turned into Swiss cheese, it felt as if her whole life had reset. There was the time before the assault where her memory was riddled with empty spaces and vague shadows, and there was the time after—when she'd stumbled into Keir Watson's arms. He was the person she'd known the longest in the part of her life she was more certain of. And his abrupt departure to chat with his partner left her feeling about as vulnerable and confused and alone as she'd been when she first woke up with her cheek in a puddle of her own blood on the cold, gritty concrete.

Chapter Three

A sharp rap at the exam room door rescued Kenna from the maddening examination of her thoughts. She turned as quickly as the ball bearings inside her skull would allow and smiled, eager to apologize for showing Keir Watson anything but gratitude. "You came back."

"I haven't been anywhere yet."

Not Keir. Not a familiar face. Her smile quickly flatlined and she backed her hip against the examination table as an older man with neatly trimmed hair that held more salt than pepper in it dropped what looked like a carry-on bag on the chair inside the door.

"Kenna, dear. Look at you. How horrible. Does it hurt?" He swallowed her up in a hug and planted a chaste kiss on her numb lips, giving Kenna the chance to do little more than wedge her hands between them and gasp in protest. "Of course it hurts. When I heard you'd been attacked..."

Kenna straight-armed him out of her personal space, pushing the older man back to get a better look at his face, hoping for a ping of recognition as he rattled on.

"…I paged the doctor. Pulled him out of a room down the hall and explained who I was so I could get a report." He squeezed her shoulders, threatening to hug her again. "He said you could have died."

"I'm sorry. I…?" Once again, it was disadvantage Kenna. *Something kick in. Please.*

The older man's eyebrows, as thick and wild as his hair was neatly cut, arched above his brown eyes like two fuzzy caterpillars. "You've forgotten me. The doctor said you had gaps in your memory—that you didn't even remember what happened to you." He covered her hand, capturing it against the front of the cashmere sweater he wore. "I'm your emergency contact. I'm the one who faxed your medical history to the hospital. It's me. Hellie."

What kind of silly name was that for a man? She tried to place the face, thinking those bushy eyebrows that so desperately needed a trim should look familiar. His skin was perfectly tanned, from too much time spent either on a golf course or in a pricey salon. And his teeth were unnaturally white. He was barely taller than she was in her bare feet, although he seemed reasonably fit for a man his age. "Hellie?" She repeated the odd name.

"Good grief, my dear, I've known you for fifteen years." Known her? How well? "Here. I'll prove it." He reached into the pocket of his pressed khaki slacks to pull out his billfold. "Here's my license, along with a picture of us with your mother and father."

"No. Wait." Kenna put a hand on his wrist to stop him. If Dr. McBride had talked to him about her condition, this man must have shown proof of a connection to her. The doctor had said she needed her memories to return to her naturally, that she needed to discover for herself what she knew and what she'd forgotten, or else she'd never be able to trust her own judgment again. "Let me figure it out."

The pungent scent of cigar smoke clinging to his clothes sparked a glimmer of recognition. He wasn't wearing a wedding ring, and she'd already noticed she wasn't, either. Not even an indentation from where one might have been stolen. Good. She hadn't forgotten a husband. But she had forgotten whatever relationship she shared with this man who thought he had the right to kiss her. Although it hadn't been much of a kiss. But perhaps the lack of any toe-curling response and spark of recognition had more to do with the anesthetic and swelling around her mouth rather than any innate repulsion. Still, she seriously hoped she could rule out boyfriend as a possibility.

The polished loafers and expensive leisure clothes reminded her of wealth. She'd been wearing a designer suit and one Jimmy Choo heel when Keir brought her to St. Luke's. So she had money, too. She was an attorney. She worked in a law firm. No, she was one of the owners of a law firm—an inheritance bestowed upon her by her father and earned through her own hard work. Bushy Brows was a partner. She pictured the letterhead on the stationery at an office desk—Kleinschmidt, Drexler, Parker and Bond—and understanding fell into place. He'd kissed her before, and she hadn't appreciated it then, either. "Helmut. You're Helmut Bond."

"Of course I am. I'd be surprised if you could forget old Hellie." Smiling, he went back to the doorway to pick up the bag. "I brought your overnight bag and insurance information and have already filled out the paperwork for you. I stashed your mail in here, too."

The man might be older, but he wasn't what she'd call old. He showed no lack of confidence, and clearly had money. Was this the kind of man she dated? She was feeling nothing like that little sting of awareness she'd felt when Keir held her hand. Was Helmut Bond supposed to mean more to her than a business associate?

Hellie set the bag on the examination table beside her. He pulled out a folder filled with papers and a sheaf of forms on a clipboard from the hospital. "These just need your signature. I took the liberty of canceling the forms you filled out earlier. These will be processed through insurance before you're billed."

Kenna took the pen he handed her, clutching it in her left hand while she fingered through the stack of letters and legal briefs bearing her name. Although she felt vaguely resentful that he had the presumption to make those business decisions for her, she supposed she had little choice about trusting that he had her best interests at heart.

Hellie tapped the form he wanted her to sign. "Are you sure you're okay? You remember how to write your name, don't you?"

"Sorry." Kenna switched the pen to her right hand and skimmed through the insurance form to make sure she wasn't agreeing to anything she shouldn't before signing her name on the bottom line.

Hellie returned the pen to the shirt pocket beneath his sweater. "Are these holes in your memory going to be permanent?"

"I don't know." She opened the file and pulled out a letter with the firm's letterhead and a space at the bottom awaiting her signature above her typed name. Images of a group of people sitting around a boardroom table flickered in her brain, and the names on the stationery began to match up with faces. A stout older man with snowy white hair—Arthur Kleinschmidt. Her father's friend and a founding partner. Hellie—regaling everyone with a story. He enjoyed being the center of attention. Stan Drexler, only a couple of years older than Kenna, sat beside her. His gaunt face and receding hairline accentuated his pointy nose, reminding her of a rat. Yes, she was remembering having that amusing observation during the weekly staff meeting. She could see the faces of the other junior partners and personal assistants who sat at the table and moved through the lushly appointed room, although some of their names escaped her.

But that meeting had been when? Last week? Last month? Couldn't she be certain of anything more recent? Like yesterday and the events leading up to the assault?

"Do you remember what happened to you last night?" her visitor asked, frowning. "Did you give the police a description? Are we going to be able to arrest the SOB and prosecute him?"

She shook her head and pulled an envelope from the file, hoping that something else here would trigger a memory. "My body says that I was in a struggle of some kind. Unfortunately, I don't remember anything about it."

"Oh, Kenna." Hellie's gaze traveled with unabashed pity over the wounds on her face. But when he reached out to touch one, she turned away to open the envelope and pull out the letter inside. "I'm so sorry. Amnesia on top of being cut up like this? Will you have scars?"

Kenna's fingers flew to the stiches and glue as she clutched the folded paper to her chest. She hadn't even thought about disfigurement. Wasn't the memory loss enough of a burden to bear?

"It's a good thing you got Dr. Colbern off that murder charge. Maybe he can repay you with a little plastic surgery." Hellie chuckled at the inside joke Kenna didn't get. "Oh, come on. Andrew Colbern? Cosmetic surgeon? His wife accused him of hiring someone to have her killed? You proved the woman wrong, of course. Made the firm a tidy sum of money."

Of course? She'd defended this Dr. Colbern? Did she make a habit of defending would-be murderers? According to a few of Keir's comments, he thought the doctor was guilty. Yet she'd gotten Colbern off. That sort of history could go a long way toward explaining why a cop like Keir Watson might consider her an enemy.

Curious to ask those questions of Keir and confirm her suspicion, Kenna set aside the papers and unzipped the overnight bag. She dug through underwear, running shoes and yoga pants inside. But as soon as she'd located the cosmetics bag and pulled out a compact, she hesitated. Clutching the small bag to her chest, she turned to face Helmut. But it wasn't the fear of looking at her reflection that gave her pause, or even his crude remark about needing a plastic surgeon. Why would a coworker be her emergency contact? Didn't she have a family? Personal friends? A boyfriend? Why had she chosen to rely on this man? Because, frankly, he wouldn't be her first choice for a confidant if this uncomfortable meeting had been their first. "How do you have access to my personal things? Are we…?"

Hellie laughed. "You and me? Oh, honey, no. It's not for lack of trying, though. After my divorce, I thought maybe the two of us could hook up…" His good humor faded. "You don't remember that, either? We've served as each other's escorts to several fund-raising events. But when I suggested we could be something more, you turned me down flat."

She had? Did he hold that against her? This guy didn't seem particularly heartbroken.

"No matter how many laughs we've shared over the years, how much we have in common, you said, as partners in the same law firm—competing for the same promotions, high-profile cases and so on—that it wasn't a smart move for your career plan to see each other socially. I've accepted that and moved on. And your decision has paid off. Once Arthur retires, it'll be you or me who takes over as senior partner. Stan hasn't brought in the big clients and built his reputation the way you and I have."

Arthur? Stan? From the board meeting. Right. "And we're not seeing anyone else?" she asked.

"I've been dating Carol on and off."

"Carol?"

"Yes, she's your…" His voice trailed off and his lips curved into a pitying smile.

"My what?" A sister? Friend?

"I don't suppose you remember her, either."

Kenna shook her head.

"You said not to tell you."

"Hellie."

"Your executive assistant. Carol Ashton. Petite brunette? Shapely. Snarky. Superefficient? You're a stronger man than I am." He laughed at his male-female ribbing. "You've always been about the work and putting that first. But I need someone in my life. You don't complicate your goals with distracting relationships. I admire that about you."

She'd let the workaholic allusion, and the fact that she apparently defended criminals and had no personal life to speak of, slide for a moment. There was a more pressing clarification she still needed here. "So you can go to my house in the middle of the night and pack my things and greet me with a kiss because…we're old friends?"

How much of a player was Helmut Bond? Had she ever succumbed to his dubious charms?

"You did get a hard whack in the head, didn't you?" Hellie put one hand on her bag. "I picked this up at the office. Carol had those files stacked with the messages and mail on your desk. You always keep a bag packed in your closet in case you work late or are running straight to the gym. Your passport was in the safe there, so I pulled that for ID. Once the call to the firm's answering service was forwarded to me, I gathered the information I thought you'd need and came right to the hospital. We share the same insurance provider, of course."

"I see." She might as well ask him to confirm a few other suspicions. "I don't have any brothers and sisters, and both my parents are dead—Kenneth and…?"

"Gloria. Yes, they're both gone." Hellie cupped a hand around her shoulder again. She waited expectantly for him to continue, hearing the seconds ticking loudly from his watch near her ear. "You're worrying me. Do I need to call a specialist for you? We have several psychiatric consultants on retainer with the firm. I could arrange for one of them to meet with you to go through hypnosis or memory exercises with you. We'd have to keep it hush-hush—out of the media so no one can question any of your recent or upcoming casework and claim incompetence and start filing appeals. I can draft a press release stating you're taking a leave of absence for your physical health after the assault. But I don't like seeing you like this."

Right. Being represented by an attorney who could be so easily distracted by the ticking of a watch, and who hadn't even remembered her own name a few hours earlier, would be bad for business. Appearing in court with her brains jumbled up like this wouldn't inspire a lot of confidence for the firm's clients. According to this man, those were liabilities that would have concerned her before the attack. But right now all she wanted was to understand who she was and what had happened to her.

"Kenna." Hellie's arms slid around her again. "Let me call someone. There are other cosmetic surgeons, other psychiatrists. If you're worried about a possible scandal, I can take you someplace outside Kansas City. I'll handle it personally."

Kenna shrugged off his tobacco-scented touch and stepped away before she realized the door was open and Keir Watson was standing there. His jacket was pulled back and his hand rested on the butt of the gun strapped to his belt. A frown deepened the angles on his face. How much of that conversation had he overheard? Had he heard the bit about her defending a man accused of murder? Or just the part about her so-called friend here claiming she needed a shrink?

As soon as she made eye contact over Hellie's shoulder, the detective pulled his hand off his weapon and strode into the room. "Dr. McBride said you had a visitor. For a second, I thought maybe Hoodie Guy…"

Was he worried her attacker had tracked her down to finish what he'd started? "I'm okay."

"Sure you are." Keir held out his hand, and Kenna deliberated for all of a nanosecond before she instinctively reached out to take it and let him pull her away from Hellie to stand beside him. "She's been through a lot tonight, sir. Maybe you should take a step back and give her time to process everything that's happened in the past few hours before you send her off to a psychiatrist and hire a spin doctor to protect your firm."

"Who are you?" Hellie's eyebrows met in an expression that was suddenly as serious as she'd expect any cutthroat attorney's to be. His gaze dropped to where she clung to Keir's hand. "This isn't a private room, son, but I can make it one."

Son? Kenna pointed a finger at Bushy Brows. "You're out of line. You owe this man an apology."

But Keir Watson didn't need her to defend him. He released her hand and took a step toward Helmut Bond. He held up his badge. "Keir Watson, KCPD. I drove Ms. Parker to the ER. I'm the one who called your office because that was the only lead I had to track down someone who knew her personally."

"Yes, of course. Thank you for calling, Officer."

"It's Detective. And you are…?"

"Helmut Bond. Ms. Parker's legal representative and friend. Thank you for your service to the community, *Detective*." He emphasized Keir's rank as though granting that concession of respect left a sour taste in his mouth. "But your presence here is no longer needed. I'll be driving Kenna home as soon as the doctor dismisses her."

Garrulous? Self-important? Allegedly dating her assistant *and* playing touchy-feely with her? Kenna had had enough. "Thank you for bringing my things, Hellie, but—"

"*I'm* driving Ms. Parker home," Keir announced.

Heat flushed the side of her face that wasn't numb from the anesthetic. "You are?" Kenna was momentarily confused by the relief surging through her, yet she seized the offer without question or apology. "I mean, he is," she stated with a little more compunction. "I feel safer with a police escort. You understand."

"Kenna, in your condition, you're hardly competent to decide who—"

"I can make my own decisions, thank you," Kenna snapped. Hellie might be a well-meaning friend, but these verbal jabs about her mental state were starting to rankle. "Detective Watson knows more about the investigation into the attempt on my life than anyone. I feel safe with him. I want him to take a look around my place and make sure everything is secure."

Despite the hard feelings he seemed to have when he'd left the room, Keir didn't have any problem following her lead and backing her up now. "I also want to confirm that it's not the primary crime scene."

"Couldn't you do that in the morning?" Hellie suggested. His brown eyes lingered on her, even though he addressed them both. "Later this morning, that is. Kenna's estate is protected by the same security company and alarm system all of our firm's partners use. If there was a break-in at her home, believe me, the police would already know about it. Give her time to get some rest and freshen up."

"Do you really think freshening up is what I'm worried about right now?" she asked.

"I'm just saying the assault didn't happen at the Parker mansion."

Was he telling her to reassure her or to force her to remember? Kenna crossed her arms around her middle, suddenly feeling very aware that the only shield she had was her hospital gown, a pair of panties and whatever attitude she could muster. She didn't have the truth on her side, because she didn't know it. And she seemed to be particularly vulnerable to every barb and innuendo Hellie uttered.

Keir might have picked up on her hesitation. Or maybe this was a testosterone thing and he simply was refusing to lose an argument to the other man. "What if her attacker disabled the alarms and security? What if it was someone she knew and she let him in? What if it was you?"

"You're walking a fine line between investigating a case and slander, Detective." Helmut Bond certainly wasn't backing down from the position of authority he claimed to have in her life. "If you want to find out the facts, do so. Do the job you're paid to do. But leave Kenna out of it."

"He'll leave me out of nothing." The backbone she'd been searching for surfaced from the cloud of fear and frustration she'd been battling all night.

Kenna linked her arm through Hellie's and guided him toward the door, winging this conversation based on the clues she'd gathered from everything the man had told her since barging into the room. "You know that I'm a driven woman. I don't wait for answers to fall into my lap. I take action. Keir is in a better position than anyone to help me with that."

"I would think you'd want a friend to rely on instead of some stranger."

"I know who I want. Detective Watson."

"At least you're sounding more like the woman I know." Helmut patted her hand where it rested on his arm.

He squeezed his fingers around hers, and she couldn't help comparing his light, smooth caress to the firm, calloused grip of Keir Watson's hand.

"Very well. I suppose it is a practical solution. What about your casework coming up next week? Anything you'd like me to tell Arthur and Stan? Anything you want Carol to put together for you?"

"It's the weekend." Between Keir and the doctor, she'd answered enough questions earlier to know she had that much right. "I'm allowed to take a couple of days off."

"You not work on the weekend?" Hellie shook his head as he opened the door. "Now I've seen everything. I thought you had a deposition on Monday to prepare for. Colbern's wife has threatened to file a civil suit against our client and the firm for emotional damages, and Arthur has asked me to step in and join the team. And though I don't really think she stands a chance of succeeding, we're on Judge Livingston's docket Thursday to go through preliminary motions. Plus, since you're the one who was working with Colbern, I'm counting on you taking that meeting with me to go over what role the firm will play when he faces the medical ethics board. I'll represent the firm's interests, of course, since he's threatened to sue, but—"

"I had my brains bashed in, Hellie. The doctor said half an inch in either of two directions and I'd be dead." More eager than ever to get rid of him, Kenna nudged him into the hallway. "I'll see how I feel Monday morning and call the office if I need to postpone or have someone else cover my appointments."

"But—"

"But nothing. I can't even think of who Judge Livingston is right now, much less what motions you're talking about. I don't remember Andrew Colbern or his wife or my assistant. And if you need me to manage your cases for you, you'll just have to wait."

His expression hardened and Kenna realized they had more of an audience than the detective watching them from inside the exam room. Did she always sound like such a harpy when she got upset? Was her impatience with Hellie a by-product of injury and fatigue? Whatever filter she'd had on her emotional impulses must have bled out with the gash behind her ear. Her nostrils flared with a deep breath and she lowered her tone to a more civil pitch and nodded to the nurse who'd helped her earlier.

Once the other woman's concerned expression eased, and she moved on down the hallway, Kenna looked to Hellie. "I'm sorry. I don't mean to snap at you. I'm not feeling like myself right now. The doctor said I'd need a few days for the swelling and headache to recede. I need to evaluate my recovery before I return to work."

Appeased by her apology, Hellie smiled. "Of course. Take whatever time you need. I just wanted you to know how valuable you are to the firm, and not worry for one moment that we don't need a woman like you at Kleinschmidt, Drexler." A woman like her? Was that a compliment or some kind of sexist remark? "My teasing about work is just the kind of tough love pep talk I'd expect from you if our situations were reversed."

She'd trade tough love for losing this headache and a little bit of TLC right about now. "Thank you for coming. Now if you don't mind, I'd like a little privacy so I can change out of this lovely hospital gown."

Kenna turned her head aside when he leaned in to give her a kiss. Was this uncomfortable feeling Hellie gave her the subconscious part of her brain trying to give her some kind of warning? Or was it simply having something come at her face, the same way she'd reacted to the syringe, that made her flinch? After a momentary hesitation, he pulled away. "I'll be in touch."

He was heading toward the lobby when Kenna re-entered the examination room. She closed the door behind her and leaned against it with a weary sigh before crossing to the exam table to gather her things. "Thanks for rescuing me again. I thought he'd never leave."

"Told you I'm keeping tabs, Counselor." Keir turned to face the table with her while she packed up the papers Hellie had brought. "Although it sounded as though you could handle him yourself if you needed to."

The burst of indignant energy she'd shown Hellie seemed to ebb with every inhale of Keir's warm, musky scent. If calming reassurance was a commodity, this man could make a fortune selling it. Feeling herself relax a little, Kenna picked up the folded letter she'd wadded in her fist and opened it to make sure she hadn't damaged an important document. Several flattened, desiccated rose petals fell out and fluttered to her feet. She looked at the parchment-colored paper, flipped it over and a vague sense of unease quickened her pulse. She had no idea why, other than this was a really weird thing to receive in the mail. There was only one symbol typed on the entire page—a capital *O* in the top left-hand corner of the paper. The rest of it was just as blank as the important parts of her memory were. "What do you suppose that means?"

"Someone's printer ran out of ink?"

"The sender wouldn't notice the page was blank before stuffing it into the envelope?"

Keir knelt at her bare toes and gathered up the petals to drop them into her hand. "Secret admirer? Maybe that's just a piece of scrap paper to contain these, and the roses are the message."

"Why would I be sentimental about dead things?" There was certainly nothing about the once red petals that had shriveled and faded with age that sparked any kind of warm feeling inside her. "I suppose these meant something to me before the attack."

Keir picked up the envelope so they both could look at it. It had been addressed to her at work and stamped with a Kansas City postmark, although there was no return address.

"The sender definitely wants to remain anonymous." Keir opened the flap for her to drop the scentless petals inside. "Did Bond bring this to you?"

Kenna nodded, stuffing the wrinkled paper inside, as well. "Everything was in the bag he brought. It all came from my office."

"Do you mind if I catch up to him and ask him about it? Maybe find out where he was tonight?"

She tilted her gaze to meet his, hearing the suspicion behind his question. "Hellie's a friend—maybe a little pompous and annoying—but he didn't do this to me."

"How do you know he's a friend? You're just going to take his word for it? The guy took his own sweet time in getting here. Made a couple of tacky comments that weren't as funny as he thought. Asked a lot of questions, too—like he might be checking to see how much you remember."

Keir's fingers closed around her arm, and she wondered at the urge to turn into the warmth seeping through the thin cotton of her gown.

"How do you know he didn't hurt you? Do you remember the face of your attacker? Was he wearing a mask? Anything about his build? His ethnicity? Whether it was even a man?"

The sensation of warmth quickly dissipated as she shrugged away from his touch. As much as she appreciated his honesty, the reminder that she hadn't been able to give him any of those details rattled her. Maybe this blind faith in Keir Watson, this feeling that she knew him better than anyone else now, was a false comfort. "How do I know *you* didn't do this to me, Detective? You said we were enemies. Maybe sending me what's left of a dead rose after cutting me up is your idea of a joke."

Instead of taking offense at standing her ground, the way Helmut Bond had, Keir grinned. "Now you're being smart. Stay that way." He lightly pinched her chin between his thumb and forefinger before heading out the door. "And I really am driving you home, so don't get any ideas about calling a cab and sneaking out of here. I'll be outside in the hallway chatting up *Hellie* for a few minutes. Then I'll bring the car around and meet you at the lobby exit when you're ready."

Nodding, Kenna closed the door behind him and crossed to her bag to pull out her clothes. It took her only a few minutes to put on the workout pants, tank top and jacket, and slip into her running shoes. It took a bit longer to carefully pull a comb through her hair without aggravating her injuries and dab on some copper gloss over her tingling lips.

With her papers and toiletries packed in the bag, she looked around the ER room one last time to make sure she had everything. Ready to leave this nightmare behind her, she hurried out into the hallway, only slowing her steps once she reached the lobby. She didn't have to worry much about curious stares because most of the people sitting or pacing among the pods of furniture had their own illnesses and loved ones to worry about. When she didn't see Keir anywhere, conversing with Helmut Bond or waiting out front in his black muscle car, Kenna perched on the edge of an empty chair near the front doors to wait.

Since she had no idea where he'd parked after dropping her off at the ER doors, she didn't know how long it would take him to walk to his car and come back for her. But the clock over the reception desk had already ticked away five minutes. Maybe Keir had gotten into another argument with Hellie. Maybe he wasn't coming back for her. Maybe putting her trust in the younger detective was the stupidest thing she'd ever done.

A nervous sense of abandonment tried to take hold, filling her shattered brain with fear and doubt. Determined not to give in to the debilitating feeling, Kenna squirmed in her chair, slowly turning her head to study the other patients and family members waiting in the lobby area. For the sun to not even be up yet, there were a surprising number of people waiting to be seen or to hear news of a loved one. Fortunately, no one seemed to notice her growing agitation—not the children putting together a puzzle with their grandmother and chatting about baby names, not the elderly couple holding hands while they both tried to read magazines, not the teenager dozing in a chair beside his texting buddy or the man on his cell phone pacing in front of the windows.

All of these people had connections to someone. All of them were absorbed in their own private worlds, oblivious of everyone else in the hospital. Kenna was the only one spying on anyone else's troubles, the only one curious enough to…

A chill rippled down her spine as if someone had blown a soft breath against the back of her neck.

She wasn't the only one watching.

Kenna spun around, immediately squeezing her eyes shut against the vertigo slamming through her skull. Several seconds passed before she dared to open her eyes. Had Keir pulled up out front? She didn't see any black cars beneath the canopy outside the hospital doors. Holding her palm against her throbbing temple, she stood and slowly surveyed the lobby. Was that…?

An afterimage of a man standing at the edge of the hallway to the ER treatment rooms imprinted itself on her brain. A faceless man in jeans and a black hoodie. Standing there. Watching her.

She blinked her eyes to focus them again, only there was no hoodie. No man, period. She glanced around the lobby again. The teenagers were both wearing hooded sweatshirts, one blue, one black. But they couldn't be in two places at once. Was she confusing them with the man she'd seen? Or imagining the picture from Keir's phone? Was her vision as addled as the rest of her brain?

Not willing to add hallucinations to the rest of the symptoms she had to deal with, Kenna hugged her bag beneath her arm and crossed the lobby to the hallway. She saw no one like the man she'd imagined here, only nurses hurrying about their business and an orderly pushing a patient in a wheelchair off the elevator. Needing confirmation one way or the other as to what she'd seen or hadn't seen, she walked down the hallway, glancing inside open doors, catching a glimpse of the empty elevator closing, wondering if the man she'd seen had stepped into a room or stairwell and shut the door behind him.

Kenna paused at the room where she'd been treated. The door stood ajar. Surely not... It would be too much...

Taking a deep breath and steeling herself for the unexpected, she pushed open the door.

Empty. Thank God. Her lungs deflated on an exhale of relief.

Until she saw Dr. McBride's work cart. The stainless steel tray had been moved across the room. And though the trash from bandage kits, hair bonnet and the saline bottle remained, someone had knocked the bloody gauze that had been there only minutes earlier onto the floor. No. There was only one lonely strip of soiled gauze lying there. The rest was missing. She checked the trash. She checked beneath the examination table.

Kenna's breathing grew shallow. Her pulse pounded against every wound on her head. This wasn't right. Something wasn't right. She doubted that any orderly had been in to clean—he would still be in here working if he hadn't cleared away everything.

Who would steal a souvenir of her blood and pain?

Who wanted that piece of her?

Who was the hooded man? "What do you want from me?"

Kenna turned and smacked into a solid chest.

Hands clamped around her shoulders and a gasp of fear stuck in her throat. She twisted.

"Kenna?"

She shoved against the trap. "Let go of me!"

"Kenna." Strong arms tightened around her. "You're shaking. What's wrong?"

She couldn't catch her breath. She couldn't think. But she could feel. Strength and warmth. She could smell. Musky and familiar. Keir. Instinct guided her arms beneath his jacket and around his waist. She pressed her face against the warm column of his neck.

Keir shifted his hold on her, sliding one hand up beneath her hair to palm the nape of her neck, and whispered against her ear, "You need to talk to me. Right now."

"I saw him. The man in the hood. The man in your picture. He was here."

Chapter Four

Keir was in trouble. He hadn't been to bed in twenty-four hours, and had endured one hell of a day at work and an emotional roller coaster of a night at the hospital. He needed a shave, some food and a serious attitude adjustment—but he didn't care. As he pulled his car into an empty lane of the highway to skirt the beginnings of morning rush-hour traffic, he tried to figure out when and how his well-ordered world had subtly shifted into this dangerous, uncharted territory. He had the why nailed down already. Scrubbing at the weary muscles at the back of his neck, he glanced over to the woman dozing in the seat across from him.

Kenna Parker was the reason why.

She was the reason he'd given up a good night's sleep, the reason he was calling in favors to get intel on an investigation that wasn't officially his, the reason he was speeding across town to take her home when he could just as easily have called a cab or even a squad car for her.

She'd torn apart the murder-for-hire case he'd put together that should have been a slam dunk, guaranteeing that he'd be having a conversation with the major case squad's lead detective Monday morning to find out how she'd bested him in a courtroom. Nobody bested him. He'd turned success into an art form. He always had a plan B or a plan C if something went south on him. He won bets and had his pick of women and solved cases with a cool blend of resourcefulness, wits and determination that had rarely failed him.

Playing savior to Kenna Parker just didn't make sense.

He wasn't supposed to like the woman who defended some of the worst criminals he and the rest of KCPD tried to put away. And yeah, it still grated on his ego that he hadn't been able to get a conviction on Andrew Colbern. Yet there was something fascinating about Kenna outside the courtroom. She was confident and self-sufficient in many ways, yet surprisingly vulnerable in others. Maybe it was just the blow to the head and slice-and-dice some pervert had done to her face that had revealed that vulnerability to him. But she seemed at such a disadvantage to egomaniacs like Hellie Bond who wanted to dictate her choices, to the perp who'd attacked her so viciously and who could, quite possibly, come back to finish the job and to that creeper who'd shown up twice now and vanished without a trace, despite a sweep of the neighborhood and hospital.

He wanted to believe that the photo he'd shown Kenna had created the power of suggestion in her scrambled brain to misidentify one of the two teenagers in the lobby who matched Hoodie Guy's description. But she was certain the boys had been on the sofa the entire time she glimpsed the man watching her and had tried to track him on her own. She was adamant not only that the man had been spying on her, but that he'd stolen a gross souvenir from her time in the ER. What kind of sicko wanted to keep the blood of his victim? This was looking more and more like some kind of obsession, because Keir imagined her attacker had kept her shoe and purse and whatever personal belongings she'd had on her at the time of the attack, too.

She couldn't be imagining the threat lurking in the shadows around her. He'd seen Hoodie Guy, too. And he wasn't about to accept it as coincidence that a man matching that description had now shown up at two locations where Kenna was. And until she regained her memory or they could find some other way to identify her attacker, every person she met was a potential enemy.

Keir didn't like those kinds of odds in a fight. Nor could he deny her sense of humor and keen intelligence that had helped her cope with it all.

Kenna was as clever and complex as Tammy had been vacuous and transparent. He'd gotten a little rush from their verbal sparring matches. And what was with his straying gaze when it should be firmly fixed on the road? Kenna Parker had legs that went on for miles, with long, lean curves emphasized by the clingy yoga pants and zippered workout jacket she wore. At the hospital, she'd held on to him as if her life depended on it, and his body had waked at the contact. His fingers craved the smooth silk of her skin. His nose sought out the cool, citrusy scent of her hair. Their bodies fit together like two pieces of a puzzle. He'd held on as long as she'd needed him to, and then for a few seconds longer because he needed to hold her. Even now his heart hammered a little harder in his chest as he remembered the imprint of her in his arms.

"You're tired, Watson," he warned himself, inhaling a deep breath and dragging his focus back to the highway. Keir glanced at the GPS on the dashboard, and busied his mind with estimating how much longer it would be until they reached the Parker Estate off State Line Drive.

He wasn't supposed to feel compassion for Kenna Parker. He wasn't supposed to have his hormones buzzing with awareness about the color of her eyes or the clinging grip of her hand or those sexy, muscular legs stretched out beneath the dashboard of his Dodge Charger.

Yep. He was so in trouble.

"You're not falling asleep on me, are you, Detective?" a softly articulate voice asked.

Kenna's eyes lit like silver with the glow from the dashboard lights. Somehow he'd missed her studying him between those long blond lashes. Right. He'd been enjoying the view farther down and fooling himself into thinking that there was something real happening between them. Conceding how distracted he was, Keir flexed his fingers around the steering wheel. "It's been a long night."

She pushed herself up straighter in her seat and adjusted her seat belt. "I'd offer to drive, but—"

"No license, no insurance card, no idea of where we're heading?"

Her concern over dangerous driving fatigue seemed to ease with the teasing repartee. "Well, I know we're in Kansas City."

"Lucky guess."

She smiled at that, then winced just as quickly. When she touched her fingertips to the line of stitches along her jaw, he suspected the anesthesia the doctor had used on her was wearing off. She had to be in discomfort if not outright pain.

He was on the verge of asking if they needed to stop for aspirin or ice packs when she leaned forward and pointed out his window to the pink haze on the horizon. "And I know we're heading south because that's the sun coming up."

"Okay, so you *do* remember a thing or two."

"I remind you that I have partial amnesia, not a case of the stupids."

It was Keir's turn to relax his concern. "No, ma'am."

"Ma'am?" She groaned. "That makes me feel old. My passport says I'm only thirty-eight. How old are you?"

He liked the *only* distinction she put on her age. "Thirty-three. And a half," he added, just to get a rise out of her.

Kenna laughed and swatted him on the shoulder. "That's terrible, Junior. Are you always this obnoxious?"

"Pretty much."

"Well, it works for you." The laughter faded as another mile passed and she leaned back against the headrest. "Why do I get the feeling my house is way out of your way? Hellie gave me the entry codes for the gate and front door, told me how to reset them once we're inside. But what if the codes don't work or you discover something suspicious? Your late night is going to turn into a long day and I've already taken advantage of your kindness and sense of duty and…"

Was she thinking about how long they'd stood in each other's arms at the hospital, too? "We've had this discussion. Driving you home is not a problem."

She rolled her head to face him and winked. "Must have forgotten that."

Keir shook his head, grinning at her ability to

handle all this with humor and class. "Now who's obnoxious?" The distinctive growl of her stomach rumbling triggered a gnawing echo inside his own belly. "Hungry?"

"I think I had a dinner meeting scheduled last night. But I don't know if I ever made it to the meeting, or if I ate anything. I couldn't even think about food in the hospital." She flattened her hand over her noisy stomach. "I'd kill for a cup of coffee, at least. Maybe we could stop at a coffee shop before we get to my house?"

Trouble reared its head again and Keir didn't resist. He needed a distraction, and so did she.

"I've got a better idea. Time for a detour." Keir eyed the cars and semitrucks behind him and pulled over three lanes to catch the next exit.

"What are you up to?" she asked.

Once he'd circled around into slower traffic, he pulled out his phone and punched in one of his favorite numbers. "I'm starving. You need caffeine." Keir had loved his mother, his sister, Sophie Collins and one other woman in his life. When the woman who had raised him and still kept house for his father and grandfather answered the phone, he couldn't help smiling. "Hey. How's my favorite girl in the whole wide world?"

"Keir?" He'd always loved Millie Leighter's laugh. "What are you up to this morning?"

"Millie, my love. Have you got a pot of coffee going already?"

Across the seat, Kenna whispered, "You're inviting me to breakfast with your girlfriend?"

"Not exactly." He turned his attention back to Millie. "I'm just coming off an all-nighter, woman, and I'm hungry for your home cookin'. I've got a guest with me, too. Is that all right?"

"Is it Hudson?" From the moment Keir had first introduced them, Millie seemed to think his bachelor partner needed a little mothering and fattening up. The fact that Hud ate up all the attention only added to her infatuation with the man.

"Not this time." He laughed. "But I'm sure he'd take a rain check."

"You know there's always room at this table for you and your friends. The more the merrier. But I warn you, your oldest brother came home late last night to hash something out with your father. And Seamus is in a cantankerous mood this morning. I don't think his physical therapy went well."

Curious, that Duff had spent the night at the house where they'd grown up instead of in his own apartment. And when wasn't his grandfather at odds with someone or something anymore? "I'll risk it. See you in a few minutes."

It didn't occur to Keir to ask Kenna if she was up for meeting a good part of his family until he'd pulled into the driveway behind Duff's truck and was escorting her up the stairs to the brick porch. "I hope this is okay. The Watsons can get a little boisterous when there's more than one of us in the room, but I promise we're a casual kind of bunch. The food will fill you up and you won't find a better cup of coffee anywhere."

Kenna finger-combed her hair over the injuries on her face and nodded. "I'm sold."

He caught her hand before she lowered it and offered a squeeze of reassurance. "You don't have to hide those. Dad raised three boys and a tomboy— we're used to seeing stitches and war wounds."

Her fingers tightened around his. "Thanks. But that's not exactly what I'm nervous about. I haven't met any of them before, have I?"

"Not that I know of."

"Good. Then I'm starting with a clean slate. I may not make the best first impression, but at least they don't know any more about me than I do them."

A level playing field wasn't too much for a woman with amnesia to ask for, he supposed. But he couldn't imagine her not impressing anyone with her tall, confident posture and those beautiful, starlit eyes. He squeezed her hand one more time before releasing her to open the storm door. "You'll be fine."

He knocked on the inside door, triggering the excited barking of a dog, before pushing it open and inviting Kenna inside.

A dark brown dog, the size of a small tank, skidded around the corner on the wood floor and collided with Kenna's foot. "Oh. Hello."

"Look out," Keir warned. The dog righted herself, then rose on her haunches to meet the new visitor. "Ruby, down. Sorry about that."

Kenna pushed the Lab mix down into a sit position and held her fist to the dog's nose for sniffing and licking, making an instant friend. "That's okay. What is she? A chocolate Lab?"

"She's something all right. Dad rescued her from the Humane Society. Ruby's half Lab, half mystery beast and half spoiled rotten."

"That's one and a half dogs." Correctly assessing that this was no kind of guard dog, Kenna scratched around the big galoot's furry ears. "Pretty impressive pedigree, Miss Ruby."

Duff Watson sauntered out of the living room, eating a cinnamon roll that smelled as if it was still warm from the oven, and Ruby immediately changed allegiance to the human with the food. "Look what the cat dragged in."

Millie hollered from the kitchen at the back of the sprawling two-story Colonial. "Thomas Watson, Jr., don't you be dropping crumbs in my clean house. And do not feed that dog."

"You're in trouble, big guy," Keir teased. "She used your real name."

Duff popped the last of the roll into his mouth and held up ten fingers to show empty hands. "What's she talking about? I didn't take any food out of the kitchen." He eyed Kenna, lingering a moment on her face before turning back to Keir. "You brought company."

"This is Kenna Parker. My oldest brother, Duff."

"I know who you are." After wiping his fingers on the front of his chest-hugging T-shirt, Duff extended his hand to Kenna. "Nice to meet you." Then he seemed to quickly dismiss her as he backed away toward the kitchen. "Millie baked fresh rolls this morning, baby bro. First come, first served." He patted his thigh for the dog to follow him. "Come on, mutt."

Once Duff and Ruby had turned the corner into the kitchen, Kenna leaned over and whispered, "I thought you said none of your family knew me."

"Yeah." Keir scraped his fingers over the stubble on his jaw. "Maybe I didn't think this through. Even if you haven't met, they know you by name and reputation. Duff's a cop, too. My grandpa is retired KCPD and Dad works as an investigative consultant for the department."

"I see. And I'm Enemy Number One to every Kansas City cop?"

Not every cop.

"Son." Keir didn't get to respond as his father came down the stairs. This time of the morning, before he'd been on his bum leg for too long, his limp was barely noticeable. "Millie said you'd called." He pulled Keir in for a hug before stepping back to shake Kenna's hand. "I'm Thomas Watson. Welcome."

"Thank you. I hope I'm not imposing, sir."

"Thomas," he corrected with a smile, then invited them to follow him down the hallway to the kitchen. "We've got a full house this morning. Saturday usually means a big breakfast around here, which means one or more of the offspring tends to show up. Come on in and I'll introduce you to everyone." He nodded to the silver-haired woman stirring eggs on the big, six-burner stove. "Good morning, Millie. Coffee ready?"

"Of course." She turned off the burner and wiped her hands on her blue apron that read If You Can't Stand the Heat, Get Out of the Kitchen and reached for Keir. He willingly wrapped her plump figure up in a hug. "There's my favorite boy."

Duff came up behind her. "I thought I was your favorite."

"I saw you share that piece of bacon with the dog, so you're on my naughty list. Now go sit down before you eat us out of house and home, and I'll put the food on the table so we can eat like civilized people."

"Yes, ma'am." Duff planted a kiss on Millie's cheek and reached around her to steal another strip of bacon.

Duff was twice the older woman's size, but she swatted his hand and shooed him out into the dining area before turning to Keir again. She reached up to cup his unshaven cheek. "Where's my handsome boy? You're scruffy this morning. You look like you haven't slept a wink."

"I haven't. Spent the night in the ER with Kenna."

Millie smoothed his wrinkled lapels, and her smile faded. "What's this? Blood?"

"Relax, it's not mine."

But in Millie's mind this was an emergency and she would handle it. She patted the crimson marks before pushing the jacket off his shoulders. "Take this off and let me spot-clean it before the stains set."

"Millie—"

"Come on, now. I insist."

"All right." Keir shrugged out of the jacket and handed it to the older woman. But as soon as she stepped toward the sink, he helped himself to a strip of bacon, too.

"Oh, you."

He grinned when she shooed him away from the counter, too.

"Your big brother is a bad influence on you. I need Niall here to keep the peace."

Keir had a feeling the middle Watson son wouldn't be interested in refereeing his brothers' misbehavior anytime soon. He grinned at the thought of his quiet, brainy brother, a medical examiner with the crime lab who'd been occupied the past few months learning a whole new set of skills as father and husband-to-be. Who'd have thought that Dr. Niall would be the first Watson brother to be getting married? Keir had always thought that Niall had the emotional range of a lamppost. But after saving his sweet, feisty neighbor and the baby boy she fostered from a ruthless killer, Niall hadn't just fallen—he'd fallen hard for Lucy McKane. Thank goodness he'd been smart enough to propose. Keir had a feeling there weren't two people on the planet who needed each other more than Niall and Lucy did.

Yep. Keir might have the moves with the ladies. But Niall had the luck. If Keir didn't like Lucy so much himself, he'd be jealous. "Niall is probably up to his eyeballs in diapers and wedding plans."

Millie folded the jacket over the crook of her elbow and clapped her hands together. "That reminds me, I promised Lucy and Niall that I'd be over to their place to babysit Tommy later this morning while they go to the mall and start registering for wedding gifts. So we'd better get this meal on the table." She reached for Kenna's hand even before introductions were made. "Where are my manners? You must be Keir's friend Kenna. How are you feeling, dear?"

"I've had better nights." She matched the older woman's smile. "But my mood is picking up already. It smells wonderful in here."

"I'm Millie. I run this household."

"I can see that. Thank you for adding one more. May I help you carry food to the table?"

"Nonsense. After a trip through the ER? You need to sit down and relax." Millie poured a mug of coffee and pushed it into Kenna's hands as if she thought their guest could use a little mothering, too. She set the platter full of bacon in Keir's hands and nudged him toward the kitchen island and the dining area beyond. "Cream and sugar's on the table. Grab the eggs and take Kenna in there and introduce her to your grandfather while I take this to the laundry room."

"Yes, ma'am." Keir led Kenna into the dining area and set the platter and bowl of scrambled eggs on one end of the long oak table. "Good morning, Jane. Grandpa." He nodded to the nurse in green scrubs with a short brown ponytail helping his white-haired grandfather reach his chair with his walker. It was good to see the family patriarch on his feet and moving, albeit slowly, under his own power. Up until a few weeks ago, he'd still been relying on a wheelchair after the brain damage from being shot had resulted in a massive stroke that had paralyzed his entire left side. Keir circled behind Kenna to pull out a chair for his grandfather and help him position himself while the nurse steadied the walker. "Kenna, this is Jane Boyle, Grandpa's live-in nurse. And this handsome old fart is Seamus Watson."

His grandfather groaned at the introduction and angled his rheumy blue gaze up at Keir while the two women exchanged a polite greeting.

Kenna nodded. "How do you do, Mr. Watson?"

"Say-moof," Grandpa insisted, his half-limp mouth curving into a shadow of his once robust smile. Despite his somewhat labored breathing from the exertion of walking to the table from his room at the back of the house, he planted himself securely beside his chair and held on to Keir's arm while he extended a hand to Kenna.

Without batting an eye at his slurred articulation or questioning what he was trying to say, Kenna quickly set down her coffee and reached out to take his hand between both of hers. "Seamus." She frowned at the scar that bisected the buzz cut of white hair along the side of his head. "Looks like you and I both have some battle scars."

Seamus's blue eyes crinkled and he released her to point a bony finger at her. "You pwettier."

Even in his fragile condition, the man could flirt. Kenna responded by tucking a feathered lock of hair behind her ear and returning the older man's crooked smile—either feeling more comfortable exposing her wounds now or putting them on display in a silent show of compassion for the injuries his grandfather couldn't hide. Keir felt an unexpected twist of appreciation and admiration in his gut, and found his hand sliding to the small of Kenna's back and lingering as he guided her into the seat next to Seamus.

The more time he spent with Kenna, the harder it was to remember just how resentful of her he'd been twenty-four hours earlier. But then, that was the Terminator with her smug confidence and razor-sharp intellect who'd burned him in court. This Kenna Parker was softer, warmer and dangerously attractive to Keir's bored libido.

When the rest of the food arrived, Keir realized his fingers were still splayed against the warmth of her back, and he quickly pulled his hand away to take his seat. Maybe some food in his empty stomach would send energy to his weary brain and clarify his wandering thoughts. He was probably confusing compassion, or maybe even gratitude at the way Kenna was engaging his grandfather this morning, with attraction. This was not a *thing* happening between them. He was a cop helping an injured woman, performing his sworn duty, doing what was necessary to safeguard a victim and stay with her long enough to hopefully come up with some sort of lead on the investigation into her attack. A cop and a criminal defense attorney? It wasn't like there was any real chance of a relationship happening between them anyway.

Once they were all seated, Thomas said grace and then Keir focused on filling his belly with Millie's home cooking and catching up on all the family news, mostly about his brother Niall's pending nuptials and adoption of the baby his fiancée, Lucy, was the legal guardian for. Despite the lively chatter, and Duff's moaning and groaning about being measured for another monkey suit and tie, Keir was aware of Jane Boyle being curiously quiet.

The thirtysomething nurse was probably about Kenna's age, although she didn't seem eager to elaborate on any of the polite questions Kenna asked in an effort to get acquainted. In between helping Seamus use a spoon for his eggs and encouraging him to pick up the bacon with his less dominant hand, Jane seemed to be disengaged this morning. She answered politely when spoken to but then drifted away into her thoughts and picked at her plate. And more than once, she pulled her cell phone from the pocket of her scrub jacket and checked it beneath the edge of the table.

Keir glanced down to the head of the table. His father had noticed Jane's withdrawal from the conversation, too. In fact, judging by the scowl lining his expression, Thomas Watson was downright irritated with the nurse. Had the two butted heads again over who was in charge of caring for Seamus and overseeing his rehabilitation? Or was something else creating tension here at the Watson household?

Keir's self-reproach and his speculation about his father were both put on hold when Millie pushed her chair away from the table. "I need to get going. Since you boys are home, I'm putting you in charge of the dishes."

"Yes, ma'am," Keir and Duff chimed in together.

"And I hung your jacket in the laundry room. Don't forget it."

"No, ma'am."

While Millie scuttled down the hallway to her room, the brothers fell into their old routine of clearing the table, just as they had done growing up. Keir encouraged Kenna to relax and stay put. There weren't that many pans and dishes to rinse and load into the dishwasher.

But when Jane Boyle excused herself to go upstairs to her room to make a phone call, Thomas got up and left the table abruptly. "I'll help."

"We've got this, Dad," Keir assured him.

But the point wasn't up for discussion. Thomas carried his plate and coffee mug to the kitchen sink. But just as quickly as he'd gotten up, he switched mental gears and grabbed his jacket off one of the pegs at the back door into the garage. "You boys finish up. I have errands to run. Is anyone parked behind me?"

Without waiting for their answers, the door closed behind him. The garage door opened and a truck engine started before Keir heard his father drive away. "What was that all about?"

Duff had watched his father stride out the door, too. "I'm not sure. But things have been tense since I got here last night." He rinsed out his milk glass and loaded it into the dishwasher. "Maybe he's just frustrated about the lack of progress on the church shooting. I know it's hard on him to see Grandpa like that. He's called in every marker he has to get some answers."

Keir handed the last glass to Duff. "He'd tell us if he found out something, wouldn't he? I mean, it's not like when Mom died and we were just kids. I know at the time he sugarcoated the true details about her murder. But we're all grown-ups now. We deal with this kind of stuff every day."

Duff dried his hands on a towel while Keir started the dishwasher. "I probably didn't help, dumping on him like I did last night."

"About what?"

"Work stuff." Duff glanced around to make sure the others were out of earshot before he nodded toward the foyer. "Meet me out there."

Keir grabbed his suit jacket from the laundry and followed Duff out to the foyer. "What's up?"

"I'm the one who should ask 'What's up?'" Duff unzipped the gym bag he'd set on the front hall table and pulled out his shoulder holster and badge. "Isn't Kenna Parker the mouthpiece who made you look like a dumb-ass on the Colbern—"

"Yes," Keir cut him off, bristling. Although he wasn't sure if he was taking offense at his brother pointing out how he'd screwed up, or at him bad-mouthing the woman who wasn't as cold and ruthless as half the department—including him—had pegged her to be. He draped the jacket over the banister and started unrolling the long sleeves of his shirt. "I'm doing my job. I found her wandering in an alley near the Shamrock Bar sometime after she was assaulted last night. The perp dumped her off there. She doesn't remember the attack at all."

"That's rough. Somebody did a real number on her." Duff slipped the straps of his holster over each shoulder and adjusted the gun beneath his arm. "Any leads?"

"Nothing useful. I'm taking point on the case for now, until somebody tells me differently. Hud's helping with the legwork." Keir shrugged into his jacket, straightening his open collar over the damp lapel. "Right now I just need to keep an eye on her."

"For medical reasons? Legal ones? Or have you got something else going on with her?"

"She's got no family to take care of her. And her emergency contact who showed up at the hospital was a self-centered prick. I wasn't sending her home with him. For all I know, he's the one who assaulted her."

Duff clipped his badge onto his belt and pulled his worn leather jacket from beneath the bag. "You got a bad vibe on this guy?"

"He was asking an awful lot of questions about what happened. And not one of them was, 'How are you feeling?' He has access to the security system at her house and told her she needed a shrink and a plastic surgeon."

"That's cold."

No kidding. "Maybe there's some professional jealousy. He's as good a suspect as anyone right now. Besides Hoodie Guy."

"Hoodie Guy?"

Keir pulled up the picture on his phone to show his brother. "He was close to the dump site and at the hospital."

"I don't see any gang colors. The neighborhood around the Shamrock is open territory anyway. Too many cops hanging out." Duff shook his head and Keir pocketed the phone. "A woman like Kenna Parker could have a lot of enemies."

"Tell me about it. It'd be nice to know where to start, though."

Duff pulled his jacket on and zipped the bag shut. "You need anything, you've got my number. I might answer."

Keir grinned at the ribbing, knowing either of his brothers, sister or father would be there in a heartbeat if he said he needed help. But he was still curious about the question Duff had dodged earlier. "What did you have to come over here to talk to Dad about?"

"I'm gearing up to do some undercover work. There's an outside shot it's related to the church shooting."

A bolt of energy shot through Keir's blood. "How so? Why didn't you or Dad say anything sooner?"

"Like I said, it's a long shot. The ATF and state police have been running down some leads on how illegal arms are getting into the city."

"Like the Mauser rifle and Glock nine mil our perp used."

Duff nodded. "They were looking for volunteers who know the area, and I was first in line. If I can find out who's selling the guns—"

"Then maybe you can find out the bastard they sold them to."

"I might be off the grid for a while. But I wanted to come up with a plan on how I could keep tabs on Grandpa's recovery and if KCPD gets any new leads on the shooting."

"Anything I can help with?"

"I'd like to use you, Liv and Niall as couriers. Dad will fill you in on the contact plan we figured out." Duff looked down the hallway toward the kitchen, as if their father were still there. "Keep an eye on him, too. Dad's worried I'm going to let things get too personal because I'm chasing down a lead on the shooting. You know what happened the last time I had a personal stake in an undercover op."

His brother had nearly died on that particular assignment. "You're smarter now, right?"

Duff grunted at the question that was both a teasing jab and an expression of concern. "I'd like to think so. But if there's a chance I can get a name on our shooter, I have to do this."

Although he hated the idea of his big brother putting himself in that kind of danger, Keir agreed. He'd do the same if he was in a position to do so. "Don't worry about things at this end. We'll keep pressing for answers on Grandpa. Let us know if you find out anything. Be safe."

"You know I'm too tough to take down."

"I know." Keir extended his hand. "Watch your back anyway."

Duff pulled him in for a hug, then pushed him away, glancing back toward the kitchen. "Watch yours. I don't know if a high-powered attorney who defends bad guys with more money than you or I will ever make is someone you want to get involved with."

"I'm not involved."

"Dude, you brought her home for breakfast. You're involved."

Chapter Five

"Sorry to keep you waiting." Kenna pulled open the passenger door on Keir's black Charger and dropped into the front seat before he could get out and open the door for her. She could tell she'd startled him. He'd been so intent on studying the image on his phone that he hadn't heard her leaving the house. "Are you looking at the man with the hood again?" she asked, nodding to the picture.

"No. It's the man who shot Grandpa."

With that bald pronouncement, the reprieve of relative normalcy she'd enjoyed for the past hour with the Watsons faded. "Did you find him?"

"I wish." Keir handed her his phone. "Duff and I were discussing the progress on the investigation—or lack thereof. This guy was no amateur. There was no DNA on any of the shell casings, and he didn't leave any other trace behind. All we know so far are the two types of weapons he used—an M-98 Mauser and a Glock handgun. KCPD has combed through a list of legal owners without anyone suspicious popping."

"What about illegal weapons?" She knew the sale of unregistered guns was a thriving business, and not every gun owner bothered to get a license.

"Duff thinks he might have a lead on that. But getting the information won't be easy. And if he can't track down the supplier, I'm afraid we'll have to wait until one of the weapons is used in another crime. Then we could at least match ballistics."

"I can see why you're having a hard time identifying a suspect. Is this your only photo?"

"It's the best one. And that's with enhancement from the crime lab." He reached over to swipe the screen back to the image of the man he'd seen lurking in the neighborhood where Keir had found her. "I sent Hoodie Guy to the lab, too, to work their magic. Even if we can't see his face, they can determine his height and see if there are any identifiers on his clothing. I don't know that he's the perp who hurt you, but I'd sure like to talk to him."

More comfortable thinking like a defense attorney than a victim who couldn't identify or discard a potential suspect, Kenna swiped her finger across the phone screen to take another look at the man who'd shot Seamus. Even if KCPD made an arrest, they'd need a lot more evidence than this photograph to convict him or even get the DA to take the case. She studied the slightly blurred image of a man in a black ski mask, wearing gloves and a long black coat. There was a handgun strapped to his waist beside a big, shiny, silver and brass belt buckle that reflected the light streaming through the stained glass windows. She touched her fingertip to the indistinct rectangle of shiny metal with something that looked like a star engraved on it, which he proudly wore as if he was some kind of rodeo champion. But there was nothing heroic about the image. He held his rifle to his shoulder like a well-trained sniper and was firing down from the balcony of a church.

Kenna's breakfast curdled in her stomach as she imagined how helpless everyone in the sanctuary below must have felt. "This guy looks like he knows what he's doing. You're lucky there weren't more casualties."

Keir shook his head as she returned the phone with the disturbing images. "I don't think it was luck. A guy with that kind of weaponry who could enter the church full of cops without being detected, and then escape as if he'd vanished into thin air? I think he did exactly what he came to do."

"Shoot your grandfather?" She looked out to the welcoming gray facade of the Watson family home, thinking how comfortable she'd been spending time there. "It's easier to believe someone would try to kill me than to harm one hair on that sweet, charming man's head."

"Hey." He started the engine before turning to her

and winking a handsome blue eye. "I'd like to keep everyone in my city in one piece, if you don't mind."

Kenna knew at least half her mouth was smiling. "Thanks. But I read the newspaper reports. There were several injuries at the shooting. Why do you think he was targeting Seamus?"

"The other injuries were from shrapnel—all minor. One lady twisted her ankle and the organist had a heart attack." Interesting clarification. Keir continued, "The guy didn't hit anyone else, and I don't believe he was a lousy shot. Maybe he was targeting our family—upsetting Liv's wedding, making each of us question every case we've worked, every criminal we've put behind bars—sending some kind of message we don't yet understand. If somebody wanted to hurt us, he certainly hit us where it would do the most emotional damage by going after an eighty-year-old man."

She hadn't helped the family's self-doubts by apparently destroying Keir's most recent case. Instead of apologizing for something she couldn't remember, Kenna focused on trying to help. "Seamus told me a little bit about the shooting. He said he doesn't remember being shot or anything that happened until he woke up in the hospital after surgery. But he told me all about your sister Olivia's wedding— how she wore your mother's veil, how you and your brothers were acting up at the altar before the ceremony started, how he knew from the sounds that the first shots came from a rifle." The older gentleman had seemed adamant about sharing what he remembered, as though he was worried he might forget the details the way she had. "Seamus has lots of time on his hands now, and has been doing a lot of reading. He was wondering if you or one of your brothers or sister could pull his case files so he could read through them instead of newspapers and books."

Keir's blue eyes narrowed. "He said all that to you? Were you interrogating him?"

Refusing to take offense, Kenna pulled her seat belt over her shoulder and fastened it. "No. I listened. If you don't rush him, he can articulate well enough to be understood. I could tell it became an exertion for him, but he seemed determined to carry on a conversation…until Jane came downstairs and said he needed to rest." As she settled more comfortably in her seat, Kenna thought about the pretty, if slightly unsociable, nurse. "Do you know what was bothering her? At first I thought it was me—that Jane thought I was expecting her to take care of me, too, or that I'd ask for free medical advice. But then I realized it wasn't resentment that had her so distracted, but concern. It was like she was expecting a call that wasn't coming—or she'd gotten a text about something that upset her."

"No clue. But you've got a good eye for details. I wanted to ask Dad about it, but he wasn't in the mood to talk."

"Maybe he's worried about her. He had a hard time keeping his eyes off her at breakfast."

"No way." Keir dismissed her idea with a shake of his head as he shifted the car into Reverse. "He was probably just avoiding an argument, since we had company. He and Jane have rubbed each other the wrong way since he first hired her—Dad's used to being in charge, and she's not used to taking orders. But Grandpa has made good strides in his recovery with her, so I think Dad tolerates her for his sake."

Kenna leaned forward to study the rays of muted sunlight poking through the low-hanging clouds as they headed east. "About Seamus…" This probably wasn't any of her business, but she wasn't one to retreat, apparently. There must be something in her personality or legal training that refused to let a subject drop until she got the answer she needed. "He was serious about wanting to take an active role in the investigation. He mentioned it three different times."

"Grandpa was a desk sergeant for most of his career. He didn't work that many investigations. He's been retired almost twenty years. I don't know who'd still have a grudge against him."

Kenna was only repeating Seamus's request, standing up for the stubborn octogenarian the way she hoped she stood up for her clients. "I think he'd appreciate whatever records you could pull for him. He wants to feel useful, like he's competent enough to help find answers for himself."

Having made her point, she sat back, turning to watch the houses and tall sweet gum trees in this older residential neighborhood pass by. Fatigue and the achy aftermath of her injuries were quickly sapping the mental boost she'd gotten from her visit with Keir's family. She was heading home to a place she couldn't remember and back to that abyss of amnesia where she wasn't sure who she knew, much less who she was supposed to trust. "I can sure relate."

Kenna startled when a warm hand wrapped around hers. She turned back to study Keir's fingers lacing together with hers, resting on the center console. He'd been a solid rock she could cling to when he held her at the hospital. But she liked this, too. It felt like such a high school thing for two grown-ups to do, but she loved the way their hands fit together, the way Keir's warmth seeped through her skin and heated the blood that seemed to rush to the place where they touched. Keir's grasp was a tangible connection to another human being, an anchor to a certain reality, while the people whose faces drifted through her addled brain seemed like ghostly shadows and vague threats she couldn't be sure were real or imagined.

"We'll find out who did this to you," he promised. "I'm going to find out who hurt both you and Grandpa."

As closely knit as everyone at the Watson house seemed to be, she had no doubt that none of them would rest until they found justice for Seamus and knew for certain their family was safe from any future threat. But Kenna wasn't holding her breath that she'd find that same kind of unflinching support from anyone at her house. Or that she could count on this kind of support from Keir for much longer. She wasn't part of his life. He was the Good Samaritan who'd rescued her. And once he'd seen her safely home, he'd go back to his family and his work, and she'd go back to the people and places that she'd forgotten, and get on with her own life.

Still, she held on to the grounding, reassuring contact of Keir's hand for as long as he was willing.

Kenna was relieved to discover that she remembered the black wrought-iron fence and the redbrick facade of the family estate as they pulled up. He'd already circled the block once, ensuring that there was no one loitering in a parked car nearby, and no hooded stranger standing among the shadows, watching for her return.

The guard shack beside the gate was empty and locked up. Keir called the number from the Weiss Security decal glued to one of the windows and put it on speaker so she could hear the conversation. They confirmed that, although Max Weiss's company electronically monitored security at the estate, the company didn't provide guards for onsite security unless specifically requested by a client. The last time any of their people had been there—beyond routine maintenance visits—was for a fund-raising event Kenna had hosted on behalf of the firm... nearly two years earlier.

Wow. Wasn't she the social butterfly? Not. Based on Helmut Bond's comments and that call, it was looking more and more like she had no personal life. Unless snubbing Hellie's attempts to date her had bruised his ego enough to want some kind of retribution. Otherwise, logic seemed to indicate that she should be concentrating on work and client issues to see who had a motive to kill her.

Keir ended the call and tucked his phone back into his pocket before entering the key code into the security pad beside the gate. He waited for the gates to slide open and shifted the car into Drive again. "Weiss has a good reputation in town. Maybe you should consider hiring one of his bodyguards until we find out who did this. At least keep someone on the premises to monitor any activity."

"You're not volunteering for the job?" The words were out of her mouth before she realized how teasing could sound like an anxious plea. The gates closed behind them with an ominous clank and Kenna jumped in her seat. Suddenly, she felt trapped, as if something or someone was closing in on her. She tried to mentally shake off the vague instinct— or was it a memory?—with little success. Maybe she hadn't been teasing, after all. She leaned back against the headrest, taking the nervous hitch out of her tone. "I'm getting used to having you around."

"These past twenty-four hours have been... interesting."

"Said the master of understatement." Kenna matched his knowing grin and relaxed a little more. Apparently, she'd been very good at being alone before the assault. She'd find a way to be good at it again.

Like the other mansions in this old-money neighborhood, the size of the two-story home with painted white columns and a black iron chandelier hanging over the front door seemed a little pretentious. Still, she loved the tall locust and pine trees, with trunks so thick she wouldn't be able to hug her arms halfway around one. There were spots of color, too, that caught her eye and made the yard feel much more inviting than the house itself. The long driveway that wound up the hill to the house was lined with hedges of spirea bushes that were budding with white and pink flowers.

The colorful splash of tiger eyes, begonias and other annuals potted in two concrete urns on either side of the front door added a touch of warmth to the cold redbrick. "This was my parents' house. We moved here when the firm became a success. My mother had all those spirea bushes planted. I remember them hosting big parties here when I was growing up."

"Do you remember being here yesterday?"

"No." She was remembering a more distant past. She shivered at the possibility that she would never be able to fill that most important blank spot of her memory.

"If things seem familiar, at least you can trust that I've brought you to the right place." Keir slowed his car in the circle drive at the front of the house, but instead of stopping, he pressed on the accelerator. "Hold on."

"The code Hellie gave me opens the front door," she reminded him.

But his blue eyes had narrowed and he was pulling back the front of his jacket and hooking it behind the holster of his gun. Keir was unbuckled before he shifted the Charger into Park in front of the three-car garage on the south side of the house and opened his door. "If everything's locked up tight, why isn't the garage?" The third door stood wide-open. She'd been looking at flowers, thinking about her mother and worrying about being alone, while he spotted a potential break-in. "Stay put. I want to check this out."

"Don't…" Her heart thundered in her chest as a forgotten fear tried to take hold. The fact that he pulled his gun and was cradling it between both hands was reason enough to wonder if he'd just discovered the scene of her attack, reason enough to be concerned about the wary cop entering the open bay without proper sight lines or backup, reason enough to find the locks on the Charger's door and secure herself inside. "Be careful," she whispered when he crept around the corner into the garage and disappeared.

Several seconds ticked by, a minute perhaps, and Kenna found herself staring at the clock on the dashboard. It was one fifteen. "One. Time is running out," she murmured, repeating the echo of a memory she couldn't quite hold on to. "There's a deadline."

What deadline? What did the number one mean? What couldn't she remember?

Kenna combed her fingers into her hair and cupped her scalp, as if she could stem the flow of memories seeping out of her head. Without Keir here to ground her, she was quickly spiraling into confusion and despair. She shifted her gaze back to the open garage door. "Hurry back, Detective."

What was he finding? Evidence of a struggle? A horrid shrine to her injuries, decorated with streamers of bloody gauze? A perp lying in wait? Finally, Keir reappeared at the open door. Alive. Unharmed. Six feet of broad shoulders and piercing blue eyes and shielding strength. Kenna released a pent-up breath, silently chastising her wandering thoughts and ping-ponging emotions. But she didn't waste any time scrambling out of the car when he holstered his gun and waved her over to join him.

"I found your car," he announced.

"My car?" Shivering at the cooler temperature

inside the shaded garage, or maybe the frissons of anxiety still firing through her system, she hugged her arms around her middle. "It's here?"

"I don't think it ever left." He pointed to the cream-colored Lexus trimmed with gold parked in the first bay. Its shiny surface and luxury appointments were a stark contrast to the paint-chipped pickup with mud and gravel caked around the tires and wheel wells parked in the open bay behind her. "You don't own this truck, do you?"

"I don't think so."

Crinkling her nose at the dank smell of churned-up soil, Kenna circled around the truck to the potting bench and workstation at the back of the garage while Keir pulled out his phone and called someone to say he wanted to run a plate number. "Your car is clean—no signs of blood or a struggle of any kind—so I think we can rule out a carjacking."

Eliminating what couldn't have happened was some kind of answer, wasn't it?

What else could the open garage and dirty truck tell them? She ran her fingers along the brightly painted ceramic pots and bags of potting soil and fertilizer stacked on the workbench. She traced the outlines drawn around the tools hanging from the Peg-Board above the bench. Something seemed familiar here among the hand shovels, rakes and pruning shears. A long, thin shape drawn in magic marker indicated a spade had once hung here. But the skinny shovel was missing. Was that significant? Was her brain trying to recall something important? Or was she just remembering her late mother's penchant for beautiful flowers and an award-winning garden that had helped turn this imposing mansion into a home? "Look how neat this work space is compared to that truck that's been off-roading. They don't belong to the same person, do they?"

"It's not registered to you," Keir confirmed, disconnecting the call and joining her between the truck and the bench. "The truck belongs to a professional landscaping company. Probably someone you hired. I don't like that whoever parked it here left the garage door open, though. There's a locked door between here and the main house. I already made sure it was secure, but still... Kenna? Where are you going?"

Her nose had picked up another scent, more pungent than the earthy dampness of the fresh mud clinging to the truck. "Do you smell that?"

"Kenna, wait."

As soon as she opened the door that led to the backyard, a gray wisp of smoke curled around her, triggering a silent alarm inside her. The trail of smoke on the early afternoon breeze was easy to follow. Was the house on fire? Jogging over the flagstone path, she darted through an open gate and followed a vine-covered arbor up to the slate-tiled patio at the back of the house. She spotted the fire that was more smoke than flame burning in a round fire pit at the corner of the patio. A few feet beyond that she saw a wheelbarrow with the missing spade and the backside of a man in a dark green shirt and muddy jeans bent over the four-foot-high brick wall that surrounded the outdoor space. He held a bucket of white paint in one hand and a large brush in the other.

"Hey, you. Sir."

The man swiped another streak of whitewash over the bricks, then wiped away part of it with a rag to let some of the bricks show through with a pinkish color. He dipped the brush into the paint again, oblivious of her approach.

"Hey!"

He startled when she raised her voice, slopping paint on the slate at his feet. He muttered a curse and set the brush in the bucket to pull a second rag from his pocket and kneel to wipe up the spill. But he didn't turn or acknowledge her as she walked up behind him.

"I'm talking to you. Who are you? What are you doing on my property?"

"Kenna, stop." A firm hand clamped around her upper arm and pulled her back a step.

"I can handle—"

But Keir's broad shoulder was suddenly wedged between her and the intruder. "I'm Detective Watson, KCPD. Sir, I need you to identify yourself."

The workman was shorter than Keir, so she didn't get a look at his face even when he stood. But she wanted to see his face, see if she recognized him as staff or a friend or maybe something terrifying. Minding Keir's cautionary stance, she shifted half a step and peered around his arm.

Not that it did her any good. The man tilted his downturned gaze to hers, but nothing about his dark eyes or the perspiration-dotted points of skin in his receding hairline seemed familiar. Maybe she'd gotten whacked on the particular part of the brain that remembered faces. That particular blank spot in her memory was worse than inconvenient.

Kenna gave her head a slight shake and swallowed a curse of her own as the man pulled a set of earbuds from his ears and let the wires dangle around his neck. "I'm Marv Bennett. Marvin. Boy, you two sure gave me a fright. I didn't know anyone else was here."

"Do you have ID on you, Marvin?" Keir asked, putting away his badge.

"Ms. Parker knows me."

She jerked her gaze up to look at him again. His face was as unrecognizable as the man beneath the shadowed hood.

"You won't vouch for me?" The man sounded surprised.

"Your ID," Keir insisted.

Since looking at the stranger working in her backyard hadn't triggered anything helpful, Kenna walked over to the fire pit. Her eyes watered at the smoking chemicals, thorny bits of stalks and charred leaves tossed in the pile of ashes. Her mind instantly went back to the letter filled with dried rose petals. Did she have a thing for roses? Were they a secret message that she and a lover she couldn't remember shared? What did that little twisting in her gut mean as she watched the plants swell and pop and then shrivel with the heat? Or was this just an unfortunate coincidence?

Kenna blinked her eyes and turned away to see the man pulling a wallet out of his pocket and showing his driver's license to Keir. There was a logo on his coveralls, but she couldn't read it from this distance. He kept his face slightly averted, in deference to the man with the badge, she supposed. "You're burning my rosebushes?"

Seeming more eager to talk to her than to the cop asking him about the truck in the garage, Marvin Bennett angled his ruddy face toward her. "I thought you'd tossed those in there. Found 'em when I came in this morning. Looked like somebody lit a fire in there, but with all the rain it didn't catch. That's why I added the kerosene." His mouth eased into a gap-toothed smile. "I figured you got impatient and started the project without me."

"What project?"

The smile faded. He twirled his finger in the air, indicating the plants around him. "Pulling out these old rosebushes. The ones we're replacing around the patio wall. You know we struggled with leaf blight last year."

She'd dug up the flowers and started this fire? When? Like the potting bench in the garage, the ruined flowers *did* seem to have some significance to her. But her stomach was queasy at the sight of the smoking plants. Was it sadness over losing something that had been so important to her mother? Was she sensing something beyond the reach of her current cognitive abilities? Or was she simply irritated that the man in charge of her garden didn't seem to be very competent, and she'd had to do his job for him? Kenna thumbed over her shoulder. "There's still some green in them. They're not going to burn."

"I could have told you that. I would have chopped 'em up and composted them. But you're the one who said you didn't want to risk the bacteria spreading to other plants."

She'd talked to this man before? His posture shifted when she didn't respond.

"Two days ago? Remember? You said you wanted this taken care of as soon as possible, but I warned you the ground was too wet to plant the new roses because we wouldn't have the proper drainage. Now, I hear your mama had a legendary green thumb, but I think you need to listen to me. That's what you hired me for, isn't it?" He tried to move around Keir, but her rescuer put out his hand to block the gardener from moving any closer to her.

Looking vaguely offended, Marvin stuffed his wallet back into his pocket and retreated a step. "You didn't call the cops on me, did you? Were the fumes getting to you? I didn't mean to bother you, ma'am. And I'd have called to tell you I was coming, but I didn't think you'd be here today."

Kenna closed her fingers around the sleeve of Keir's jacket to remove the blockade and stepped up beside him, appreciating his effort to protect her, but needing answers almost more than she needed to feel safe. She tucked her hair behind her ears, deciding which question she wanted to start with. But the gardener's mouth rounded with a soft whistle before she could speak. "Oh, wow. Ms. Parker, what happened to you? Are you okay?"

For a while there, she'd forgotten the damage done to her face. Hating that others could be so distracted by her unfortunate appearance, she quickly feathered her long bangs back over her cheek and forehead. "Why didn't you think I'd be at home?"

"You always go into the office on Saturday mornings. When you said you wanted the project handled ASAP, I just assumed that as soon as the rain let up a bit, I could…" The man stared at her face long enough that she ended up averting her own gaze to the pattern of light gray and charcoal threads running through the shoulder of Keir's jacket. "I can come back another time to finish up. I wanted to get those new rosebushes planted before the soil got too muddy. Weatherman says we're supposed to get more rain tonight and tomorrow. You sure got a lot of stitches. Were you in a car accident?"

Kenna hugged her arms around her middle and turned her face completely away from his curious concern, feeling her breath lock up in her chest at the wave of helpless self-consciousness sweeping through her.

But Keir's smooth, authoritative voice took up the interrogation she couldn't continue. "How long have you been here today, Mr. Bennett?"

"Since eight thirty."

"If that's your truck, you must have seen Ms. Parker's car in the garage. Why didn't you think anyone was at home?"

"Yeah, I thought that was weird, but, well, the house was dark—shades were drawn on most of the windows. I've been here all morning and nobody said boo to me. Ms. Parker almost always comes out to talk about the garden if she's in. You know how she likes to be in charge."

Kenna's chin came up at what almost sounded like an insult. But Bennett chuckled and lowered his voice to a whisper. "Besides, it isn't my business to be too curious about where a pretty lady spends her nights. I'm sure she spends them with you, of course," he added hastily, as if the thought that she or Keir might be offended came a few words too late. "I didn't mean to imply anything."

Keir wasn't laughing. He didn't correct the man's assumption about spending the night together, either. "How long have you worked at the Parker Estate?"

"Couple of years. That's how long I've worked for Riley Greenscapes, at any rate. I guess they've been mowing the grass and taking care of the yard here a lot longer than that." A defensive note crept into his tone as the questions kept coming. "Hey, I'm not asking for overtime because it's Saturday. As long as I put in my hours and I'm not disturbing the household, I've got permission to be here. We have a contract to do regular upkeep of the yard and garden."

That didn't make sense. The suspicious attorney in Kenna found a strength the depleted woman couldn't seem to hold on to. She peeked around Keir's shoulder to look directly at the gardener. "Then why are you painting?"

Marvin shifted on his feet with an embarrassed chuckle. "Well, um, no offense, ma'am, but when you pulled out the old bushes, some of the ground must have settled behind it. I guess the roots and weathering over the years dislodged the mortar holding it together. This section here was all tumbled down when I came here this morning. I didn't want you to hold me responsible, so I put it back as best I could and replaced the dirt, but I couldn't get the bricks to all line up like before, and some of the red was peeking through. Thought if I painted it, you wouldn't notice the difference. I found the paint and brush out in the garage. Like I said, ma'am, I didn't even know you were here. I'll put out the fire if that's bothering you." He picked up the shovel, scooped up a spade of dirt from the wheelbarrow and tossed it onto the smoking yard waste. "And I'll get that wall finished right away."

"Your repairs look fine." When had she worked in the garden? Was it a hobby of hers? An homage to her late mother? Or was she such a tyrant that she'd attempt to complete the job herself if the hired help couldn't get it right? Kenna's headache seemed to be coming back. She rubbed at her temple. "Have you seen or heard anyone on the property or in the house?"

He tossed another shovel of dirt onto the dying flames. "I just told you I hadn't."

"You didn't see a man wearing a black hoodie?"

"No. Why?"

Keir didn't bother to explain. "How did you get onto the grounds if no one was here to let you in?"

Marvin stabbed the spade into the dirt in the wheelbarrow and rested his elbow on top of the handle before turning. "Am I in some kind of trouble?"

"How did you get in?" Kenna repeated.

"I've got the company's passkey to get through the gate and into the garage." He reached inside his green uniform shirt and pulled a lanyard with a key card from around his neck. "It's not like I'm here casing the joint, wanting to rob it. I'm doing more than

I'm supposed to here. I've never had one complaint from a customer about using my passkey privileges, I swear. You can check with my boss, Mr. Riley."

"We will," Kenna and Keir chimed in together.

Less and less surprised to find out how well their drive complemented each other's, Kenna looked up. The faint shadows beneath Keir's eyes and the day-old beard stubble added a tough edge to his chiseled features and indolent grin. She had a feeling it hadn't been an easy task to discredit him on the witness stand—Keir Watson was intelligent and observant, dedicated to uncovering the truth and protective of the people he represented—traits she believed she shared. She liked teaming up with him a lot more than she imagined she'd enjoyed facing off against him in court. Her heart beat a little faster in her chest when he winked a silent message of support at her, and she wondered if she'd ever felt this inexplicable burst of excitement, this empowering sense of feeding off someone's intellect and energy, with another man in the life she'd forgotten.

Marvin interrupted her speculation before she could come up with an answer. "Ma'am, is everything all right? You never did say how you got hurt. You don't think I had something to do with it, do you?"

Kenna's nostrils flared with a deep breath of the damp air upwind of the fire pit. Hormonal rushes aside, she was exhausted. She needed to be in better shape, both physically and mentally, to pursue this investigation any further today. And while she hadn't been entirely satisfied with the gardener's answers, she had a feeling that the man would only grow more defensive if she and Keir kept pushing.

Apparently, Keir agreed. "I'm just doing my job, sir—talking to anyone who might have seen something."

"Seen something? Are you saying she got mugged?" he asked Keir. "Some kind of home invasion? In *this* neighborhood? Should I not be here by myself?"

"I think you're perfectly safe, Mr. Bennett," Keir assured him. "However, do you think you could come back Monday to finish this job? Ms. Parker really needs her rest."

"Well, as long as I don't get blamed for the job not being done." The gardener wiped his forehead with the back of one of his work gloves. His brown eyes were focused squarely on her when his face reappeared. "I didn't mean to upset you, ma'am. If it isn't raining too hard, Monday will be just fine. You're not going to file a complaint with my boss, are you?"

"No." She dredged up half a smile. Of course he'd be worried about his job after being grilled by a cop and an attorney, and then being asked to leave. "I appreciate your flexibility. Thank you."

While Marvin tossed more dirt into the fire pit, Keir's hand slid to the small of her back, turning her toward the double French doors lining the patio.

He nodded to the keypad. "Can you get inside from here?"

"We'll find out." Kenna pulled the paper from Hellie out of her jacket pocket and punched in the code. Nine-six-four-two-one. The glass door unlocked, but her fingers hovered over the keys without pushing the door open. "One isn't the right number."

"Sure it is. It's open... Kenna?"

She looked up into the narrowed focus of Keir's blue eyes.

"That's what you said when you stumbled out of the alley last night."

"I did?"

"Yes. You couldn't tell me what it meant then. Are you remembering something now? If *one* is wrong, then what's the right number?"

Dozens of numbers cycled through her brain—big numbers, small numbers, numbers in every type of graphic she could imagine. A chalk drawing. A neon sign. Markings on a plastic syringe. The time on a digital clock, ticking away. She tried to latch on to one of those numbers, tried to make all the counting stop, tried to make sense of any of it. "I don't know. I keep feeling like I'm on a deadline, like I'm going to miss something important if I don't remember it. But then..." She shook her head. "There's nothing there."

"A one o'clock appointment? A trial that starts on the first of the month?"

"I don't know!" she snapped, more irritated with

herself at not having an answer than at Keir for prodding her with questions. She drew in a calming breath and repeated in a more civil tone, "I don't know."

Besides, the phrase that kept playing in her head was that one was the *wrong* number. So neither of Keir's suggestions could be the answer.

When she turned her gaze back to tell him so, she saw that they still had an audience. A very interested audience standing there with a brush and pail of white paint in his hands. "Mr. Bennett. I thought we'd dismissed you."

He set the paint and brush inside the wheelbarrow before answering, "I was worried, ma'am. You sure you're all right?"

No. I'm frightened out of my mind and afraid I'm completely losing it. But out loud, she answered, "I'm fine."

The warmth of Keir's hand moved across her back. "You go on in. I'll get rid of him. I want to scout out the grounds, make sure no one snuck in by some other route. It'll be a while before I come back. Lock up behind me."

He leaned in and gently pressed a kiss beside the stitches at her temple. Kenna gasped, though whether it was surprise at the tender contact or the chill she felt when he pulled his hand away, she couldn't tell. She couldn't ask about that reassuring little kiss, either. She tilted her gaze to briefly meet the deep blue of his eyes, but Keir was turning away as if sharing that kind of intimacy with her was his right, and as normal and natural an occurrence between them as breathing.

He strode across the patio to the gardener. "Bennett, you're coming with me."

Chapter Six

Overwhelming fatigue rushed in as Kenna locked the door and rested her forehead against a cool pane of glass. She watched the two men disappear from sight along the path back to the garage and still she couldn't bring herself to move.

The only part of her body that seemed alert were the nerve endings still dancing with a newly discovered delight where Keir's mouth had caressed her. Tiny strands of her hair had caught in the coffee-brown stubble of Keir's beard and she'd felt a dozen ticklish little tugs across her scalp as he moved his lips over her skin. She could recall each individual sensation as if it were happening to her at this very moment and savored it. She could recall just as clearly the heat of Keir's arms closing around her, absorbing her panic and filling her with comfort and strength. Even now her body warmed at the memory of his fingers gently caressing the nape of her neck and sifting into her hair, and her small breasts rubbing against the harder planes of his chest as she pulled herself closer. She remembered breathing in his spicy masculine scent from the skin beneath his shirt collar.

Kenna's gaze wondered over to the freshly turned earth and potted roses lined up and ready to be planted along the top of the patio wall. Every detail about Keir Watson was tattooed on her brain. But why couldn't she remember the conversation she'd had with Marvin Bennett? Why couldn't she remember dinner or who she'd met or why she'd gone out yesterday in the first place? Why were faces from the distant past so much clearer than the friends and business associates and staff she must have interacted with over the past twenty-four hours or so? Was her brain truly as bruised and battered as her face? Or was Dr. McBride right, and she was subconsciously trying to shield herself from a memory so shocking and horrible that she'd never remember anything pertaining to the attack?

And how vital was it for her to start recalling those details? She couldn't help thinking that giving her amnesia and a new look hadn't been her attacker's goal. Would she even know she was in danger if he or she came back to finish the job until it was too late?

And why had Keir Watson kissed her? Did she look like she was on her last leg and he'd felt sorry for her? Was he making a point to Marvin Bennett that the lady of the house was protected? And why did she keep trying to imagine what that kiss would have felt like on her lips? It seemed as if answers to the important questions weren't coming this afternoon.

Pushing away from the door, Kenna noticed the skin print she'd left on the glass and pulled the sleeve of her jacket down over her hand to wipe it clean. "Hmm."

As beautiful and inviting as the wide patio with the tall oaks, colorful flowers and rock paths beyond might be, she apparently didn't take the time to enjoy them as she should. There wasn't another mark on the wall of windows and doors, inside or out, no fingerprint on any of the knobs. Didn't she or anyone else ever go out and sit in the sun or walk the shady paths? Did she ever prop a door open to let a cooling spring breeze into the house? What a waste.

Turning into the carpeted entertainment area, with a wall of built-in cabinets, a fireplace and a flat-screen TV above the mantel, she strolled through the long room to the marble-topped island and pristine white kitchen on the other side. Maybe she didn't cook, either. There wasn't a mark on any of the stainless appliances, and the only thing adorning the countertop besides a display of lemons and oranges was a handwritten note beneath the cordless phone on the wall.

Kenna scanned the note about weekend meals left

in the fridge by someone named Renata and waited for a familiar image to form in her brain. Nothing. Agitation stirred in her blood as she set the note down and moved on to reacquaint herself with her house. Pushing open a swinging door, she entered a formal dining room with twelve chairs around a long cherry wood table. Beyond that, she passed through a squared-off archway into the marble-tiled foyer.

Here there was a fresh-cut bouquet in a tall crystal vase on a side table beneath a mirror. Opposite that hung a large painting of the mansion, when it had been draped with red, white and blue bunting for a patriotic holiday. She peeked into a study with a desk surrounded by floor-to-ceiling shelves filled with books.

"My father's office," she murmured out loud, remembering the tall windows and leather couches. A second door revealed her mother's office—with lighter-colored woodwork and paint, the shelves filled with gardening and decorating books instead of legal tomes. The other rooms on the first floor were set up for entertaining but were so spotlessly preserved she wondered if the reception a year and a half earlier that Weiss Security had mentioned when Keir called them was the last time she'd had guests in the house. Either that or she'd hired a wicked-good cleaning staff. Maybe that Renata who'd left salads and a casserole for her was Superwoman.

"I live in a museum," she murmured, thinking the

house was as cold and sterile and empty as the Watson home had been filled with noise and love and living. What kind of person chose this sort of life? Was she really the workaholic Helmut Bond had claimed? Maybe that was why no one had come looking for her in the hospital besides an associate from the firm who'd had to be paged by an answering service. The more she discovered about her life, the less she was liking the woman she'd been.

She heard the growling noise of a diesel engine starting up. Marvin Bennett was probably driving away. Soon, Keir would follow, and she'd be all alone in this well-appointed mausoleum.

That unsettling thought made her breath lock up in her chest. This house seemed to indicate that she was very experienced at being alone. The idea should have given her comfort. If she was alone, she wouldn't have to worry about the disadvantage of not knowing someone on sight. She wouldn't have to be afraid of failing to recognize her attacker. But *alone* sounded very...lonely right now. Kenna tilted her gaze up the central, polished walnut staircase with a runner of Oriental wool. "Maybe I live upstairs."

But the bedrooms and baths up there were just as spotless. Clean. Beautiful, like live-screen captures from a home decorating magazine, but stagnant, cold. Kenna found the room she thought was hers, a fact confirmed by the business suits, dresses and shoes stored in the walk-in closet. A chest of drawers revealed just how finicky she was at sorting her jewelry and lingerie by color and design. Dressy stuff up top—more casual at the bottom.

"This is nuts," she said out loud. How boring, regimented, guarded and uptight could one woman be? Was all this perfection some sort of defense strategy? Had she felt some other aspect of her life was beyond her control? She didn't think her parents had been harsh taskmasters. Beyond remembering the high expectations they'd had for her, she recalled long conversations at the dining room table and numerous trips they'd taken together. Had something happened more recently that had made her go all scary control freak on the place she called home?

In the bottom drawer she found several colorful items that had been folded up for so long, the clothes had creases in them. She pulled out a pair of cotton lounge pants in royal blue. They were decorated with old-style London police boxes printed in a bright turquoise color. Kenna smiled and hugged the pants to her chest, feeling a twinge of relief. Somewhere along the line, she'd had a sense of fun. She had a kitschy obsession with British television.

Why wasn't she fun anymore?

Why was she so alone?

Who had done this to her? Or perhaps a better question to ask was why had she done this to herself?

Rebelling at the stringent restraint that seemed to have dictated her life before the attack, Kenna tossed the pants onto the four-poster bed and pawed at the comforter, freeing the pillows and blanket underneath and raking them together into a pile in the middle of the bed. "That's better."

Slightly breathless, and secretly satisfied at the hint of anarchy in her overly organized world, she went into the small bedroom next to her own that had been converted into a home office, complete with barrister cases, a couch and a treadmill desk set up in front of another TV. If work was her thing, maybe she'd find something here that would make her feel more at home than the rest of the mansion had. Kenna opened the drapes and sat at the traditional Chippendale-style desk near the window.

Other than a pewter tankard filled with ink pens and mechanical pencils, there was nothing but a framed photograph of her and her parents sitting on one side of the blotter, and a cordless telephone propped up in its cradle on the other. The red light was blinking on the answering machine, drawing her attention to the numeral 5, indicating the number of messages recorded on the machine. She snorted a wry laugh. "Maybe that's the right number." Wondering if she'd recognize any of the voices or names, Kenna pushed Play.

She opened drawers and searched through the contents of her desk while a woman identifying herself as Carol came on the line. Remembering the name Helmut Bond had mentioned, Kenna tried to put a face to her assistant's friendly voice. "Hey, Kenna. You weren't answering your cell, so I thought I'd leave a message on your landline. I'm guessing you're already at your meeting with your friend Barbara Jean." Barbara Jean?

Kenna pulled out the yellow legal pad she found in the main drawer and jotted down the name. *Barbara Jean?* Was that who she'd met for dinner? Had she ever made it to that meeting?

"Just wanted to remind you that I'm leaving early today for my class reunion, but I've got the correspondence typed up and ready for you to sign on your desk, along with the files you requested on those old cases. I also wanted to give you a heads-up. Congrats on winning that case this morning, but I've already fielded a wild, surprisingly colorful call from Devon Colbern, Dr. Colbern's wife. Pretty sure the woman was drunk. I saved it in case you need a recording for evidence."

"Evidence?" Kenna whispered out loud while the message continued.

"In polite terms, she's not thrilled with the outcome of the trial and holds you personally responsible for everything that's wrong in her life." Kenna's assistant laughed. "There's a message from Andrew Colbern that isn't much better. Instead of being grateful that you kept him out of prison, he's worried about what the divorce and civil suit is going to cost him. He said you should have found a better way to clear him of charges than to blame the police for not doing their job."

Kenna's stomach was twisting into knots. That was why Keir considered her an enemy. Was blaming the police—apparently Keir, in particular—the only way she'd been able to defend Ddr. Colbern? Just how many people hated her, blamed her, had a reason to want to hurt her? Did she like these people she represented? Did she really believe in their innocence and thought she was serving justice? Or was she just all about winning her case and making money? That reputation could certainly earn her plenty of enemies.

"Anyway, that's it," Carol finished. "Have a good weekend. See you Monday."

After a beep, the second message began to play. But there was nothing recorded but a few seconds of silence before there was a hang-up and the recorder beeped again. Probably just an automated call or a misdial.

Kenna ignored most of the third message as Hellie's voice came on the line. Goodness, the man loved the sound of his own voice. While Carol's message must have come yesterday afternoon before her attack and the trip to the hospital, Helmut Bond wished her a good morning and was following up to make sure she'd made it home safely. If she needed anything, she was to call him. He'd be there in a heartbeat. Better yet, why didn't she come stay at his house so he could take care of her? Kenna frowned. What would Carol have to say about her boyfriend inviting another woman over while she was away at her reunion? Yet, if they were a couple, why hadn't Hellie gone to the reunion with her?

But while he poured out two-faced platitudes, Kenna's attention was fixed on the legal pad.

"What is that?" She turned her pencil onto its side and shaded over the indentations that had been left from a page that had been torn away. The echo of an earlier message soon emerged. *"Talk to Arthur? BED file."*

Talk to the senior partner about what? When had she jotted this note? What bed? Whose bed? Why would she talk to Arthur Kleinschmidt about a bed? She'd written the letters in all caps, so maybe they were an abbreviation or acronym.

Kenna opened other drawers, looking for any file or flash drive labeled *BED*, in case it meant something significant. She looked for some kind of address book, too, hoping to find a last name for the Barbara Jean friend she was supposed to meet. About the only thing she did find was a wall calendar folded up in the bottom drawer. It was a souvenir from what she supposed was her insurance agent. But neither the company nor the agent was named Barbara or had the initials BED. With no success here at the main desk, she got up and went to the treadmill to boot up the laptop sitting there.

She clicked on various icons. No BED file here, either, but she did find a folder labeled Contacts and opened it to scroll through the names of what must be clients and business consultants. She found phone numbers for members of the firm and her assistant, Carol. But, of course, they were listed by their last names, so she scrolled through each one line by line, searching for anyone named Barbara. An unhappy message from Andrew Colbern played like white noise in the background while she let the cursor hover over someone named B. J. Webster. There had been other *B* names. Could one of them be the Barbara Jean she was supposed to meet? And how smart was it to call up someone she couldn't remember out of the blue and ask if she knew Kenna Parker? She'd sound crazy, for sure, and might possibly be tipping off her attacker, or the person who'd set her up to be killed.

Until she could decide the wisest course of action, Kenna shut down the laptop and moved on to inspect the barrister cases. Everything inside was as annoyingly organized and neatly arranged as the items in her bedroom had been.

Everything, that is, except for stack of envelopes wedged beneath a law dictionary. Kenna opened the glass door and lifted the heavy book to pull out the odd packet of letters.

After another beep, the last message played. It was another automated call. Kenna turned the envelopes, tied together with a wrinkled ribbon, over in her hand and gasped.

Feeling an uncomfortable suspicion licking at her pulse, she carried them to the treadmill table and untied the ribbon. The stationery was familiar, an identical match to the plain beige envelope she'd opened at the hospital. Suspicion grew into apprehension, kicking her heart rate up a notch as she leafed through the stack. The postmarks were all from Kansas City, each dated seven days apart. Each had been sent to her office, and not one had a return address.

Swallowing hard to keep the tension in her gut from rising into her throat, she opened the oldest envelope and pulled out the letter inside. She unfolded it. Three brittle rose petals fell out. A brief message was typed across the top. *Your DEADline is in 147 days.* "Deadline? What deadline?"

If this was a reminder for a journal article or legal brief she had to write, why keep it hidden away? Why would she ever write herself a letter like this instead of making a notation on her calendar or phone? Did she have 147 days to get the house ready to sell or lose twenty pounds or enter some kind of competition? Maybe the rose petals meant she planned to enter a flower show?

She opened the second envelope. There were only a few words typed there, too, and more petals. *You have 140 days until your DEADline.*

The third one was similar. A piece of paper holding the remnants of a faded, dried-out rose. A terse message was typed across the top: *133 days left.*

The next one mentioned the number *126*. The next, *119*. Then *112*.

Kenna stopped reading.

The letter that Hellie had delivered this morning at the hospital—the symbol on it wasn't the letter *O*. It was a zero.

These letters were some kind of terrifying countdown.

Kenna snatched her fingers away as if the paper had cut her.

These weren't souvenirs from any lover. She dashed back to the desk and pulled out the calendar to check the dates. She opened the calendar on top of the desk and recoiled. Every date had been marked through with an *X*. From the date when the first letter had arrived until yesterday. She'd been counting down the numbers, too. Today's date had been circled half a dozen times. Today was the deadline. Today was zero.

And then she realized that the last message was still playing. Only, it wasn't silence at all. Someone was breathing on the long recording. The caller inhaled a stuttering breath from time to time, fighting to control exertion. Or emotion. Someone was there, listening, waiting for her to pick up.

Kenna slowly turned toward the disturbing wheeze of breath on the recording. She was in trouble. All this meant something. The calls. The missing BED file and meeting with the mysterious Barbara Jean. These haunting, terrifying letters. Someone had been threatening her for months before the attack. Had she been afraid before the assault? Because she was damn certain she was afraid now.

The creepy breathing faded away into a growly whisper of noise until the voice finally spoke. "Your time's up. The deadline is today. I'm so sorry about yesterday. It wasn't supposed to happen like that. But I'll see you tonight."

Stone-cold dread filled her veins. The breathing grew more ragged again, as if the anticipation of meeting her excited the caller. Kenna hugged her arms across her chest and backed away from the cruel taunt. Dead. Line. "He's coming back to kill me. Tonight."

Another telephone rang in the background. She heard a muffled curse and a hasty scramble before the recording suddenly went dead.

How could a phone ring when the caller was already on the line? None of this made any sense. And she desperately needed something to make sense.

A sharp rap of sound startled her. Kenna screamed as the noise dragged her from her miasmic thoughts. Shaking inside her skin as her pounding pulse tried to regulate itself, she glanced around the office, fighting to orient herself in the here and now.

"Kenna!" She heard pounding at the front door. A

blessedly familiar voice shouted, "Kenna? It's Keir. Open up or I'm breaking in."

Before he knocked a third time, Kenna bolted out of the room. "Keir?" She ran down the stairs, hurriedly punched in the security code and swung open the door. "Keir!"

She saw shoulders and a gun before an arm snaked around her waist and KCPD Detective Keir Watson dragged her away from the open door. "You screamed."

"I did?"

"Yes." He shut the door behind him and twisted the dead bolt. He was still pulling her with him as he peeked into the dining room and her father's office. "Is somebody here? Baby, what's wrong?"

"Don't call me baby. I'm not two years—"

"Then tell me what's wrong!"

Kenna instinctively recoiled from the harsh command.

Keir released her and raised his hand in apology. "Ah, hell. With no sleep I've got no filter in me. I'm—"

He started to apologize, but she waved his softer tone aside and cut the distance between them. "No. You're right." Bracing her palms against his chest, she looked straight into those questioning blue eyes. She was still too panicked to be very polite herself. "Don't be nice to me right now. I need you to be a cop." Her fingers fisted in the front of his jacket and she pulled him to the stairs. "It's a countdown."

"What's a countdown?"

"Just come with me. I need you to see this. I need you to hear. Please."

When he nodded, she released him and hurried up the stairs. Keir followed, right on her heels. "Counselor, you're scaring me."

"Join the club." She led him past her bedroom to her office. "In here."

Keir grabbed her wrist and pulled her back so he could enter first. After a quick survey, he holstered his gun and crossed to the scattered letters and pile of rose petals on the treadmill desk. "Explain to me exactly what happened."

Assuming he considered it safe enough for her to enter, Kenna cued up the fifth message on the answering machine and started talking.

"The numbers. They're a countdown." She talked about the spotless house and the mysterious Barbara Jean and BED file, the weekly letters she'd stashed away and the caller who seemed to think she ought to be dead. Bursts of angry frustration and soul-deep fear peppered her rambling words. "One is the wrong number because I was supposed to have one day left. Today is day zero. Today is when he planned to attack me. I think he's coming to kill me."

"Who?"

"I don't know." She slapped at the calendar on her

desk. "Clearly I was keeping track long before the attack. Someone was stalking me." She applauded Keir's muttered curse when he listened to the vile message. "I think that's why everything is so freaking perfect in this house. Because that's something I can control. It's a classic response for dealing with abuse or a stalker. And I don't have the injuries to indicate abuse—Dr. McBride looked at my medical records and—"

"Did you report it to the police?"

"I don't remember." She hugged her arms around her waist. "Would it have done any good? Aren't I the enemy?" Keir's gaze had fixed on her, following her as she paced across the room. "Someone has been threatening me, and maybe…maybe I wasn't scared enough for him. I'm too stubborn and independent…" But even her emotional rant was running out of steam. She was breathing hard as she stopped in front of him to meet those blue eyes. "My parents raised me to be that way. And I work in a tough field, a man's world, and…and…" Kenna swayed with exhaustion and fell silent.

"Can I be nice to you now?" Keir's voice was deep-pitched, calm.

All she could do was nod. He turned her into his arms and led her into the hallway, away from the grim secrets of her home office.

Once he'd put some distance between her and the collection of threats, he stopped and let her lean back against the wall to rest. "It's a good thing you're such a strong woman. I can't imagine anyone else still standing after all you've been through." His tone was as gently hypnotic as the stroke of his fingers through her hair. And then his hand stopped, cupping the side of her neck and jaw. She didn't realize how chilled she still was until she felt the warmth of his palm seeping into her skin. She didn't know how much she needed to see the honest desire darkening his eyes. "Don't sue me for this."

Keir leaned in and pressed a soft, chaste kiss against her lips. He lingered for a moment, long enough for Kenna to reach up and wind her fingers around his wrist. They stood like that for several seconds, lips gently touching, warming each other. She felt the strength of his pulse beating beneath her thumb, felt her own pulse leaping against the heat of his hand.

When he pulled away, Kenna felt bereft. Keir's chest expanded in a deep sigh that matched her own. His gazed dropped to the quivering pout of her lips. With no trace of anesthetic to numb them, she'd felt every moment of that kiss. She felt how cold they were now without his touch. And then his feet parted slightly, his fingers tightening against the sensitive nape of her neck.

A hand at her back pulled her body into his, imprinting her with a hard chest and belt buckle and even a badge against her belly. Kenna tilted her chin, her lips already parting as Keir closed his mouth over hers.

As tender and sweet as that first kiss had been, this one was hungry and bold.

Kenna tasted coffee and salty bacon on the tongue that speared between her lips and danced against hers. Keir's mouth was a heady mix of demand and request, daring forays and soothing retreats. He was careful of the stitches close to one side of her mouth, but took his sweet time exploring the rest. Kenna's pulse pounded in her ears. The shock that had chilled her body melted away, and a different sort of adrenaline poured like honey into her veins. She needed this contact, this realness, and drank in everything he offered as if it was her life's blood she needed to survive.

She stretched her body against his, reaching up to cup his jaw between her hands. She felt the rasp of his day-old beard tickling her palms and fingertips and sensitized lips. There was a needy moan and a satisfied catch of breath, although she couldn't be sure if the sounds were Keir's or hers or belonged to them both. A very feminine response tingled in the tips of her breasts as he walked her back against the wall, his chest rubbing against hers, his muscular thighs crowding her own.

The kiss blotted out every fear, every doubt, leaving only this moment, this man, filling her head. This scorching connection they shared had been an inevitable spark between flint and steel, waiting to be struck from the moment he'd first swept her up in his arms and carried her to his car. Keir Watson looked like sin and danger all rolled up into a tailored suit. He matched her verbal sorties zing for zing, and grounded her in a world that was safe and secure. And the man could flat-out kiss a woman like he meant business.

Kenna was as mindless with passion as she'd been with panic a few minutes earlier by the time Keir angled his hips away from hers and eased some space between them. She still clung to the sandpapery angles of his jaw as he rested his forehead against hers. His mouth hovered above hers, his warm, panting breaths caressing her kiss-stung lips.

"So that got out of hand." He braced his hands against the wall on either side of her head as if he couldn't risk touching her right now. He studied the marks on her forehead, cheek and jaw and, a moment later, brushed her hair aside to study them more closely. But she sensed concern rather than any kind of repulsion in his curious perusal. "You're a strong woman, Kenna Parker. But in some ways you're as fragile as glass. I didn't hurt you, did I?"

Kenna looked up into eyes of deep, rich blue. "Not a bit." She eased her grip on his face and pulled her arms down between them. She curled her fingers into the nubby wool of his jacket, feeling slightly saner as she sagged against his chest. "You're a good kisser, Detective."

"So are you, Counselor." A deep sigh stirred the crown of her hair and he straightened, folding his arms protectively around her. "Believe me, so are you."

He must have felt her breath steadying, sensed some of her strength returning after a few moments, because he tipped his head back from hers, rubbing his hands up and down her arms. "I'd like to say that was unexpected, but—"

"You just never expected it to happen with me."

"Honestly?"

"Always."

"No." Thankfully, the man didn't mince words or speak in riddles, giving her one more reason to trust him. "I don't want to be enemies anymore. But I know we're going to face off in a courtroom again one day, and we're going to try to prove each other wrong. You're going to piss me off by being such a damn good attorney, and I'm going to side with KCPD against you every time."

Kenna nodded, hating to agree. "There are a lot of reasons why you and I wouldn't work. A lot of potential conflict down the line. A lot of gossip behind our backs, maybe some unfriendly accusations."

His hands stopped their soothing massage and came to rest on her shoulders. "This isn't the time to try to figure all that out." He pressed a kiss to her temple and pulled away altogether. "Time to get to work." He strolled back to her office and punched in a number on his phone. "I'm calling the lab. We're analyzing everything."

A bit of the panic returned as he walked away. When he moved on down the hall toward the stairs, she hurried after him. "Keir?"

He stopped at her bedroom door and flipped on the lights to peek inside. "Don't worry. I'm not going anywhere."

He checked the closet and en suite and locks on the windows. Kenna waited in the doorway until he moved on to inspect the next room. Even though he was talking on the phone, she followed him, reasoning out the practicalities of why he needed to go as rationally as she would argue salient points in front of a judge. "But you should leave. You have a life. I'm just this crazy woman who stumbled into your arms, and you've been too kind to walk away. There are other cops in this city who are willing to help me, right? They can't all hate the *Terminator* so much that they wouldn't do their best by me." She couldn't help noticing the weary shadows beneath his eyes as he faced her in the doorway and ended the call. "You haven't slept. Your family needs you."

"I'm the first officer on the scene, so I have to call this in, no matter what. It'd be a hundred percent more efficient if I'm the one to report our observations and suspicions instead of you having to go through everything that's happened all over again with someone new." He pocketed his phone before pulling back the front of his jacket and splaying his hands at his waist. "Do you want me to stay?"

Kenna imagined a clock slowly ticking off the beats in her head as she debated between what was smart and what felt right. What was a little pride or worry over losing her independence in the face of mind-numbing fear and loneliness? She offered him a wry smile. "Desperately."

An answering grin appeared on his sexy mouth and he held out his hand to her. Kenna laced her fingers together with his and he took her with him as he secured the rest of the upstairs rooms. Then they headed downstairs and he repeated the security sweep on the lower floor and basement.

Keir was still holding her hand after the team from the crime lab had taken pictures and packed up the evidence from her office and left. Kenna was dead on her feet, but she insisted that she be kept in the loop on any information the police found. Her fingers were still linked to Keir's as his partner, Hud Kramer, gave them a rundown on the information they'd been able to assess thus far.

The short, stocky detective with wavy brown hair pulled a notepad from the pocket of his blue chambray shirt and opened it. "We dumped the LUDs on Ms. Parker's phone. The first unidentified call came from a disposable cell at about three p.m. yesterday.

We assume that call came in before the assault—maybe he was verifying your location—that you were en route to your meeting. Maybe that's what prompted you to leave your home and its security system in the first place—you thought you were going to put a stop to the harassment. You've gotten a call from that number every day this week, different times of the day and night. But we can't trace it."

Keir leaned his hip on the stool beside the one where she sat at the kitchen island. "What about that last call? That had to come after the attack. You're not telling me there are two different perverts out there, getting their rocks off at Kenna's expense."

Hud hesitated. He glanced from his partner to Kenna and back to Keir.

Kenna didn't need any soft sell of the facts. She needed answers. "Where did the last call come from?"

"The number is registered…to you."

"How is that possible?" she asked.

Keir stood, muttering a curse as if he already knew the answer. "The perp took her purse."

Hud nodded. "Whoever that is…he called from your cell phone."

Chapter Seven

Keir walked with his brother Niall around the outside of the Parker mansion, checking that the house, garage and yard were secure. Even though the driveway and buildings were well lit, the two men carried flashlights. The clouds rolling in overhead blocked out the moon and stars, leaving plenty of shadows between the iron fence and house where an intruder could hide.

Kenna and Niall's fiancée, Lucy McKane, were inside, getting better acquainted, cleaning up after the enchilada casserole they'd shared for dinner and watching over Tommy, the foster baby Niall and Lucy were adopting after their autumn wedding. The couple had brought over a bag with a change of clothes, toiletries and his phone charger so Keir wouldn't have to leave the estate just yet. Going on thirty-eight hours without sleep, Keir felt better about having another set of eyes on the premises for a while. Niall wasn't much of a conversationalist, and when Kenna had politely asked about their wedding plans, he jumped at the chance to join his younger brother as Keir suggested he wanted to make sure everything was secure before the storm hit.

The two men had made their way back to the slate-tiled patio before Niall, a medical examiner with the KCPD Crime Lab, finally spoke about something other than the weather and Keir's security concerns. "Do you think they're still talking about wedding showers and bachelorette parties in there?"

Keir grinned. "Are you all planned out?"

Niall turned his light into the trees out back while Keir walked around the patio furniture to circle the perimeter of the painted brick wall. "I suggested an elopement, but Lucy has never had the chance to be part of a big family event before. She's so excited about including all of us, I didn't want to disappoint her."

"She's hard to say no to, isn't she?"

Fortunately, Lucy was as outgoing as Niall was introverted. Keir couldn't think of any two people who complemented each other more. She brought him out of his esoteric shell, and he grounded her in a sense of security and belonging the woman had never known.

"I've tried," Niall admitted, adjusting his glasses to peer into the darkness beyond the flower garden. "It's not a statistical impossibility, but on this project it has been particularly difficult." He swung his flashlight over to Keir. "By the way, I don't know what you and Duff are planning, but there are to be no strippers at my bachelor party."

Keir laughed out loud. "Is that coming from you or Lucy?"

"Lucy and the victims on my autopsy table are the only women I ever want to see naked." Niall raked his fingers through his hair. "That didn't come out right. Of course I never want to see Lucy on my table."

Keir laughed and gave his brother a teasing punch on the arm. "It's a good thing that woman loves you. I don't know how you'd ever catch anyone else."

Niall peered down at him through his glasses, giving him that stop-being-a-wiseass look, before deftly changing the topic. "So you're staying the night with Kenna? Aren't you supposed to be off the clock this weekend?"

"Yes. And yes." Keir expected some kind of teasing or curious follow-up question about letting things get too personal. Duff or Millie or someone had no doubt filled his brother in about bringing Kenna to the house where they'd grown up, making it clear to someone with even half of Niall's intellect that he'd turned an off-duty rescue into a 24/7 investigation and bodyguard commitment.

But teasing wasn't Niall's way. "Good. With a head injury like she has, it's a good idea that someone stays with her."

"Not to mention the guy who wants her dead may come back tonight to finish the job."

"True. Or maybe that countdown is all about making her *think* he's coming tonight. That would be a pretty terrifying way to get in her head."

From everything Keir had observed, the perp had done an exemplary job of that. But Kenna was stronger than the creep could ever imagine, and he couldn't imagine her allowing that fear to defeat her.

Their lights converged on the wall Marvin Bennett had been painting earlier that day. The top three rows of bricks were bulging out like a potbellied stove as the ground settled behind them. Keir touched one with his fingertips first to make sure the paint had dried; then he handed his flashlight to Niall. "Here. Hold this."

He tried to push the bowing wall in with his hip, and when it barely budged he bent down and put his shoulder into it. Niall set the flashlights on top of the wall and added his strength to the effort. But he pulled away when it became clear it wasn't going to be an easy fix and vaulted over the top of the retaining wall. He knelt between the roses waiting to be planted and put his brain to work instead, scraping aside some of the loose dirt and shining his light down behind the wall. Catching on to what his brother was doing, Keir removed a few of the loose bricks to see if this was a simple repair they could take care of so Kenna wouldn't worry about it, or if she'd need to call a professional.

Niall eyed the potted roses on either side of him. They all had double containers from the nursery, so he picked one up and pulled off the extra plastic pot to use it as a makeshift shovel. A minute later he stopped digging and sat back on his heels. "That's good ol' Missouri clay down there at the bottom under the potting soil. With all this rain, the water's gotten behind the wall and expanded it into a solid mass. You'll have to dig that out with something stronger than a plastic pot."

But Keir was less interested in his brother's soil assessment than he was in the dark red smear staining the underside of the brick he held in his hand. "Hey, Niall. What do you make of this?"

Niall jumped down to the patio and shone his light on the faded whitewash. "Looks organic. It's not rust-colored enough to be the clay. Look at the corner where it's chipped away. I'd say it's blood."

"That's what I thought." An uncomfortable scenario was forming in Keir's head. This brick had been turned upside down and freshly painted. How long had that stain been there before the gardener had covered it up with his botched repair? Keir turned to look inside the house. The first-floor rooms on this side of the house were all lit up, and he could see through to the kitchen where Lucy was pouring a mug of coffee while Kenna sat at the island, playing with the baby in his jump seat on top of the counter. The two women seemed to be enjoying their conversation. Keir turned away from their laughter and looked up at his brother. "Is it Kenna's?"

"There's no way to tell unless I analyze it. It could belong to the mason who built the wall, or any worker or guest. Could even be from an animal." Niall took the brick to study it at another angle. "The sample looks degraded. It's been out in the elements. But brick is porous enough that it could absorb the serums. Possibly, there's a purer sample deeper inside, beneath the paint."

Niall started to hand it to him, but Keir pushed it back into his brother's hands. "Can you take that to the lab and analyze it?"

Niall glanced inside the house, too. "You think this is Kenna's blood?"

"I think I haven't found the original crime scene yet. She was in a fight somewhere. Why not here? This is as good a lead as anything I've uncovered so far."

Niall nodded. "If she was cut here, too, there should be more blood. Directional splatter from the knife or scalpel or whatever instrument was used."

"If the perp had time to dump Kenna downtown, then he'd have the place to himself and plenty of time to clean up." He tilted his gaze to the overcast sky. "And Mother Nature hasn't exactly been kind to crime scenes."

"I'll grab my kit from the car and bag the brick. I'll get some luminol and my ultraviolet light to see if I can pick up anything else out here." He hesitated a moment before leaving. "You know, even if this is her blood, it could have been left by an earlier injury. Could I take a look at her head wound? See if it's consistent with striking the wall?"

"We can ask. I imagine she'll say yes. She's as anxious to find answers as I am."

"We need to get Tommy home and put him to bed. But I can drop him off with Lucy and head out to the lab tonight."

Keir extended his hand to his brother. "Thanks. I'll owe you one."

"No, you won't." Niall hooked his thumb around Keir's and shared the bros' handshake. "You were there for me when Tommy's birth father tried to kill Lucy. I figure I still owe *you*."

TWO HOURS HAD passed since Niall and his new family left the estate and Keir locked it down tight. Kenna had given Keir his pick of guest rooms upstairs and he'd settled into the one across from hers. It hadn't taken him long to unpack, but he'd indulged a few extra minutes in the shower. The hot water and shave had gone a long way to unkinking his weary muscles and washing away the grit of the day.

Before he turned in, he pulled a pair of jeans on over his briefs and padded across the hall in his bare feet. He nudged open the door to Kenna's room to see for himself one last time that she was safe before he turned in. The room was pitch-dark except for the sliver of light from the hallway, but it fell over the top of her four-poster bed and he could see that there was no blond head of hair resting on either pillow.

Feeling a twinge of alarm, he pushed the door wide-open to verify that she wasn't sitting in a chair with a book or in the adjoining bathroom. No light under the bathroom door. That didn't necessarily mean…

And then he heard voices downstairs. A man's voice mostly. "Ah, hell."

Had that creep called Kenna again? Was someone here? Was he making good on his zero-hour threat?

Keir dashed back into his room to get his gun and raced down the staircase toward the muffled conversation. Front door locked. Lights off. He'd given himself fifteen stupid minutes to clean up and feel halfway human again, and that was all the time it had taken for someone to get into… He burst into the kitchen to find it empty. A light was on over the stove. "Kenna?"

He saw her sitting in the middle of the family room in front of a big-screen TV. That and the lamp on one end table provided the only light in the room. Keir's alarm quickly fizzled into annoyance when he realized the voices he'd heard were coming from the television. Kenna held a mug in her hand and was reading something on the computer screen in her lap.

"Everything okay down here?" he asked, wondering what had her so mesmerized on that computer that she hadn't answered when he called out to her. Just to appease his own peace of mind and let the adrenaline that had charged through him earlier run its course, he crossed behind her to check the back doors to the patio. All secure.

He spared a few moments to study the flashes of lightning in the clouds whipping through the night sky. A storm was coming. Breathing normally again, he tucked his Glock into the back waistband of his jeans and came back to the tan sectional sofa. Kenna sat cross-legged in the middle. She'd wrapped a cream-colored afghan around her shoulders and had her laptop computer open on the knees of her royal blue pajama pants.

"I brewed a new pot of coffee." She finally spoke, pointing toward the kitchen without taking her eyes off the words scrolling across the computer screen. "Changed it over to decaf if you want some."

Keir considered pouring himself a cup of the fragrant brew, but he wanted an explanation first. He crossed his arms over his chest and waited for her to look up. "Is there some reason not answering and scaring me seemed like a good idea? Is everything okay?"

She closed out the page she was reading and

glanced up. Her silvery eyes widened with surprise. "You're half naked—you shaved." She took her time gazing her fill of his shoulders and chest before she turned away. He'd never realized how a woman's hungry look could be such a turn-on. Instead of acting on the desire arcing between them, however, she dialed the intimacy back a notch and opted for the clever banter thing they shared. "That's a good look on you." She thrust her long legs out from beneath the cover and scooted forward to set down her drink and grab the remote from the coffee table. "Did I wake you? Sometimes the sound effects get a little loud."

"I was getting ready to turn in when I realized you hadn't gone to bed."

"I needed to do a little work." She pointed the remote at the television and turned down the volume several notches until the characters running around on-screen were barely whispering. "I turned that on for background noise. Besides, if tonight is the deadline, and he's coming for me—"

"You don't want him to take you by surprise. That's what I'm here for." Keir moved to the far side of the table to face her. Even in the flickering light from the television, he could see the bruises on her pale skin and the fatigue lining her eyes. "Why haven't you passed out yet? Dr. McBride and my brother both said sleep would be good for you."

She tucked a swath of damp, straight hair behind

her ear and tilted those moonlit eyes up to his. "I don't know how long I was out the last time I lost consciousness. Long enough for the man who did this to think I was dead and haul me downtown and leave me in a filthy alley. Maybe I'm afraid the next time I go to sleep I'll never wake up again."

Keir plucked the computer off her lap, moving it beyond the grasping hands that tried to take it back. "And maybe you're too much of a workaholic." He sat down beside her and pulled the laptop onto his thighs. "What are you working on?"

"I'm reading through old case files. My personal notes on them, anyway. I'm assuming copies of the actual paperwork, trial transcripts and so on are kept at the Kleinschmidt, Drexler offices."

While Keir skimmed over the icons on her screen, Kenna picked up the steaming mug of decaf and cradled it between her hands. "I'm a horrible person. Look at that list of people I've defended. Andrew Colbern. The Rose Red Rapist. Jericho Meade's nephew."

A community leader who'd rather commit murder than pay for a divorce, a serial rapist and a mobster wannabe who'd made a bid to take over his uncle's criminal empire. Two of the three had been convicted, but Brian Elliott was serving at least forty-two years with consecutive sentences, and Austin Meade was serving a life term instead of facing the death penalty, thanks to Kenna.

Her pale gaze stared at the fireplace beneath the television, and Keir wondered what dark place her thoughts had wondered to. *A horrible person* seemed like a pretty harsh condemnation for a woman he was quickly growing to care about. He even felt a pinch of guilt at the *Terminator* nickname he'd once tossed so casually around the precinct offices. "Maybe you're doing a service to Kansas City."

She blew a snort of derision across her coffee. "Yeah, right. If you can afford her, Kenna Parker will defend anybody."

Keir scrubbed his fingers over the smooth skin of his jaw, thinking how he wanted to say this. "We need good criminal defense attorneys. You make sure those trials are fair so that when we put the perpetrators away in prison, they stay there. No one can argue an appeal and get them back on the streets because you've already given them the best defense possible."

She set the mug down and turned to him. "That's a pretty speech, Detective. You almost make me sound like one of the good guys."

"It's the truth." The more he thought about it, the more Keir believed what he was saying. He just hadn't bothered to see the whole picture of what a trial looked like before now. "Think of it this way, when I arrest a perp, I want him to go away because the department proved he committed a crime and that he deserves to be locked up. I don't want to win because you're lousy at your job—I want the guy to know we did our job right and we nailed him."

She pulled the afghan more tightly around her shoulders. "Maybe I should become a victim's advocate. The police would like me better, and I'd certainly be able to relate to my clients now. I wonder how much pro bono work I used to do. It might be good for my conscience, if not my tough-chick image, to do more pro bono work on the victims' behalves."

"You representing the little guys? Wow. It's something to consider. But only if it's what you want to do."

She sank back into the sofa beside him. "I don't know what I want."

"That's because you haven't slept in two days."

"I wonder if I used to know—in my life before I forgot faces and days and…"

The wistful despair in her voice pricked at something tender and protective inside Keir. He needed to hold her. He needed to do something to help her or he was going to have to go for a very long run in the rain. But what did a woman he'd only known for a couple of days need from him? He lifted the computer off his lap. "Everything saved?"

She nodded and he shut it down and set it on the coffee table. When he leaned back, his heavier weight shifted the cushion and she tilted toward him. Her shoulder bumped his. And when she rested her cheek against him and breathed a heavy sigh, he didn't mind that he'd booked it down the stairs, fearing the worst, and she hadn't responded to his shouts. Her hand drifted over to rest on his knee and they watched the muted show together for a few minutes before Kenna curled her legs up on the cushion beside her. Keir stretched his arm across the back of the couch and she snuggled up against his chest. Nope. With that clean, citrusy scent of her shampoo filling his nose and the heat of her long, lithe body warming his side, Keir didn't mind, at all.

Thunder rumbled outside, rattling the windowpanes on the patio doors. Kenna shifted, resting her back against him and pulling his arm down over her stomach like a second blanket to watch the first drops of rain fall. He tried not to notice how his forearm was tucked beneath her breasts. Maybe it was all the electricity in the air outside that made his skin tingle, but even through the crocheted afghan and cotton knit of her pajama top, the small, pert mounds teased the hair on his arm with every inhale of breath.

The first wave of gentle rain quickly passed. Then sheets of water poured down, drumming with a growing fury against the slate and glass as the wind picked up. A streak of lightning forked out of the sky, followed a second later by an answering crack of thunder. "Your brother must have worked out there for an hour."

Keir's nostrils flared with a frustrated sigh. "And the only useful trace he found was the blood on the brick."

"But he thinks the shape of the wound at the back of my skull is consistent with hitting the sharp corner on that wall. Do you think out there—right outside my own home—is where I was attacked?" Her breasts swelled with a deep breath against his forearm. "That means my attacker was someone I know—someone I thought was a friend, or someone I was meeting because of work. I wouldn't let a stranger through the gate, would I?"

"I doubt it."

"Do you think Niall will find an answer that can help me?"

"He may be able to determine that you hit your head on the brick, but between all the rain and Marv Bennett's handiwork, any other evidence we might have found out there is probably nonexistent." He tried to concentrate on the conversation, but she kept toying with his fingers until he splayed them out. She slipped her fingers between his and he gently closed his grip around hers, hoping she found comfort, assurance and the unique connection they shared in this simple contact the way he did. "We probably won't even be able to prove it was anything more than an accident that you hit your head."

"I didn't trip and fall and get these hash marks on my face."

"You haven't sent those letters or made those phone calls, either. But a good attorney would want us to prove cause and effect. And right now we can't prove that the harassment and your injuries are related."

"Really?" She squeezed her hand around his in a gentle reprimand. "You're throwing the attorney card at me?"

"No. I don't want there to be any doubts." And then he whispered a vow. "I want the guy who hurt you to know we nailed him."

He pressed a kiss to the crown of her hair and wrapped the other arm around her. He turned, scooting his back against the pillows. He lifted her onto his lap, stretching his legs out beneath hers on the long couch. Just as their hands fit so perfectly together, just as their mouths had meshed in those kisses upstairs, Kenna fit his body as if hers had been made for him. Their toes touched as their legs tangled together. Her bottom nestled against his groin. Her long, lithe back leaned back against his chest, and her head rested on his shoulder, allowing him to simply turn his cheek to rub it against the softness of her hair.

His body was reacting to this quiet intimacy. Something deeper inside—something protective, something hopeful, something warning him of what he could have—what he could lose—was reacting, too. Another woman, another time, another circumstance, and he might have acted on the arousal simmering in his veins and swelling between his thighs. But right now there was no other woman, there was no other time that mattered. He'd loved and lost a woman before because he'd taken too long to admit what he felt. But in the short span of time he'd known Kenna Parker—really known her—he was more certain that this was something serious than in the two years he'd been with Sophie. Maybe the difference was being a young buck hungry to establish himself as a success outside his older brothers' shadows—and being a mature man who'd seen enough of the ugly side of life to know that if he wasn't comfortable in his own skin, then he'd never be happy anywhere.

But that was a lot of thinking, a lot of feeling and wanting and fearing, to make a smart decision right now. So Keir ignored the messages his body and heart were sending and stuck to the conversation about his investigation. "I'm just pointing out that we haven't gathered all the evidence we need to make a case yet. The jerk who did this to you still has the advantage of anonymity—unless that blood somehow turns out to be his. Even then he'd have to be in a database somewhere to be identified."

"What if I have to spend the rest of my life wondering if I know that face? What if I pass him on the street or meet him in the courtroom or at a cocktail party, and never even know I'm looking my attacker in the eye? My coworkers? My clients? The people who work for me? What if I think he's a friend and

I blithely follow him out of a room, and he pulls a knife to finish what he started? I'll never see the threat until it's too late. If I never remember what happened, he'll always have the advantage over me." The moan in her chest was almost a cry of sorrow. "I can't imagine how I'm ever going to resolve those kinds of trust issues with people."

She squirmed in his lap at the disquieting thought and Keir hugged his arms more securely around her, pressing his lips into her fragrant hair. "Do you trust me?"

After a moment, she nodded, stirring her hair against his mouth and releasing that heady fragrance. "I think so. As much as I can anyone right now."

"Then trust me when I tell you that I'm not going to leave you until this guy is caught and behind bars."

With that vow, she pushed his arms away and scooted onto the edge of the sofa so she could turn and face him. "You have to go back to work on Monday. You can't promise me twenty-four/seven. Even if the storm or you being here keeps him away tonight, he'll try again. And chances are you won't be here. What if it takes days to identify him? Or months? Years? What if I never—"

He caught her face between his hands, carefully avoiding the marks on her cheek and jaw. "He's never going to hurt you again, Kenna. I promise you that."

Gray eyes locked on to his, searching, deciding. And just as he thought she was going to nod or say she had that much faith in him, or even argue that he was being unrealistic, she pulled away, spinning toward the coffee table. "Wait a minute. The BED file. That's not the name of the file. It's the name of the person."

Keir tried to keep up with the abrupt change in topic. "You know someone named Bed?"

She picked up her laptop. "Initials. *Brian Elliott.* There's no *D* in his name, but I did defend him. Maybe it means *Brian Elliott Defense.* I don't remember his face, but I remember the trial. The newspapers nicknamed him the Rose Red Rapist because he left a rose with each of his victims. Could the rose petals have something to do with me representing him? He always claimed he was innocent."

Keir pressed the top of the laptop back down when she opened it. "He was caught in the act, attempting to rape a woman he'd abducted. She's now married to the cop who rescued her. They both made extremely reliable witnesses."

"Yes, well, the man's delusional and completely sociopathic. He doesn't have to really be innocent to be upset that I didn't get him off at his trial."

"The man is in prison." Keir moved the laptop back to the table and pulled his phone from the front pocket of his jeans. "I can call and confirm it if you want. But I'd have gotten a department-wide alert if he'd escaped. Elliott didn't do this to you."

"Has he made phone calls? Had any visitors?"

She touched his wrist as if he kept that kind of information on his phone. "The man is a billionaire. He has plenty of assets to hire someone to do his dirty work for him."

"I'll request the communication logs from Jefferson City. They'll fax them to the department tomorrow." Keir pulled up his contacts and scrolled through to find a number for the prison office. The assistant warden wouldn't be there, but he could leave a message requesting the information. "I'd have to get a court order to look into his finances."

"I need to see that BED file." If Keir was exhausted, he knew that Kenna had to be running on fumes. Still, while he placed the call, she jumped up and hurried to the phone in the kitchen. He watched her pick up the receiver, but pause with her finger on the keypad. Frustration at obviously forgetting the number she wanted to call was evident in the sag of her shoulders. But the woman was nothing if not stubbornly resilient. She replaced the phone in its cradle and pulled open a drawer to retrieve the phone book. She muttered out loud as she flipped through the pages. "It's probably at work. I can call Hellie to borrow his keys or let me in until I get my set replaced. I know we keep hard copies of completed cases on file. I need to see a list of Elliott's known contacts." Keir ended his call and followed her to the kitchen. "Maybe a witness who testified against him or one of his surviving victims—"

"Kenna." He closed the phone book and pushed it to the back of the counter. When she started to protest, he cupped the uninjured side of her beautiful face and brushed the long damp bangs away from the wounds on the other side. "It's midnight. People are sleeping. You should be, too. You need to rest. And heal. Elliott's not going anywhere. You can call Bond in the morning and I'll drive you into the city to your office."

"It's midnight?"

"Yeah. The deadline's passed."

She nodded, then shook her head. "Just because nothing happened doesn't mean…"

He feathered the heavy silk of her hair between his fingers and tucked it behind her ear, letting his hand linger against the warm pulse at the side of her neck. In one moment he was soothing her manic energy; in the next, he was dipping his head and claiming her mouth in a sweetly drugging kiss. Even as he tasted the soft, full curve of her lower lip, even as he teased the seam of her mouth with his tongue and she welcomed him into her warm, decadent heat, he sensed her energy flagging. Her hands settled at his waist, singeing his bare skin, igniting the impulse to pull her onto her toes and bury his tongue inside her mouth, to bury himself inside her body and surround himself with her heat.

But this wasn't the time to give in to the passion that sparked inside him. The hour was late, the woman was exhausted and the danger was still out there, lurking, stalking, waiting for the opportunity to strike again. With a reluctant groan, Keir pulled his mouth from hers. He planted one more soothing kiss on her lips, another in her hair. Then he pulled her into his arms and cradled her head against his shoulder. Her arms snaked around his waist and she relaxed against him with a contented sigh.

"I'll be with you while you sleep," he promised. "And I'll make sure you wake up in the morning."

"That'll be another one I owe you, Detective." Her lips tickled his skin as she spoke.

He squeezed his eyes shut at the unintended caress and tried not to notice the tips of her breasts beading against the plane of his chest or the way her fingers splayed across his spine. He hoped she didn't hear the hitch in his breathing when she adjusted her stance to snuggle closer, inadvertently stroking across his own sensitive flesh and coaxing his nipples to proud attention. "Told you, I'm keeping tabs."

"Send me the bill." She tried to give the teasing right back, but her mouth opened in a big yawn that blew a whisper of warm breath across the hollow of his throat. And yeah, that touch triggered a little crazy inside him, too. But what surprised him more was the almost painful grasp of tender heat squeezing around his heart.

And that was the impulse he acted on.

"Come on." He reached down to hook a hand

behind her knees and swung her up into his arms. "No more brilliant ideas or arguing with me tonight, okay? We can catch the bad guys tomorrow."

She wound her arms around his neck. "Promise?"

"You're like a dog with a bone." He wasn't sure if that was a kiss or a smile he felt against his throat, but he'd treasure either one. Keir carried Kenna back to the couch and tucked her in with the afghan. He picked up the remote and pushed the volume up again before settling into the cushions beside her. "Now tell me all about this time-traveling doctor and why you're so fascinated with him."

"Well, if you had a Scottish accent, you'd remind me a little of…"

Her voice trailed away and she was gone. Relieved to see her finally succumb to much-needed sleep, Keir turned off the television. He pulled his gun from the back of his jeans and slid it beneath the end pillow. Then he stretched his legs out beneath her on the sofa, draped the afghan over them both and, while the storm outside thundered around them, surrendered to sleep.

Chapter Eight

"Thank you, Hellie."

Helmut Bond met Kenna at the curb with an umbrella as she climbed out of Keir's car in front of the high-rise building housing the Kleinschmidt, Drexler law offices in downtown Kansas City. With his arm circling her back, the older man held the umbrella over their heads and dashed inside the main lobby of the building, leaving Keir to drive on down the street to find a parking place as if he were nothing more than a chauffeur to her.

She'd survived a 147-day countdown to a dire threat that she suspected had happened one day early for some unknown reason. But the fact that the presumably connected assault was out of sync with her stalker's meticulous timeline, and the fact that she was still alive, made her believe the danger wasn't over by any stretch of the imagination. Until she could either remember her attacker or piece together enough circumstantial evidence to identify him, she wouldn't be able to shake the fear that must have plagued her every waking thought for the past four and a half months.

"I was coming in anyway this afternoon to meet with a client."

"A client? On a Sunday?"

"He was free. I was free. He said he'd be in the city, so I gave him a call." Hellie stopped on the mat inside the door and shook the excess water off the umbrella and the shoulders of his trench coat. "I was hoping for a break in the weather, though."

Kenna wiped at the spots of rain on the sleeves of her navy blue geometric-print sweater set and the knees of her skinny jeans. A few moments later, Keir shoved open the glass door behind them and joined them. He straightened the collar of his black KCPD jacket that he'd turned up against the curtain of rain falling outside and shook the water out of his hair, spraying both Kenna and Hellie.

Kenna smiled at the boyish disarray of sleek dark hair spiking out in a dozen different directions, but Hellie wiped a spot off his cheek and grunted. "I see the police department is still offering you protection."

Irritated with Hellie's condescending tone, and simply because she wanted to touch it, she reached up and combed her fingers through Keir's short, wet hair, smoothing it back into place. *That's right, Hellie. Keir Watson means a whole lot more to me than just the hired help.* "Yes, Detective Watson has been taking very good care of me."

Keir winked as if he understood the point she was making for the other attorney's benefit. Hellie must have observed the personal interaction, too, because his tone didn't change. "I'm glad to know my tax dollars are being put to good use. Shall we?"

Keir wrapped his hand around Kenna's and gestured toward the bank of elevators. "By all means, Mr. Bond. Lead on."

Once inside the first elevator, Hellie pushed the button for the fifth floor. "I must say you're looking better than you did a couple of nights ago at the hospital. You actually have some color in your face—and I don't mean the bruises." He chuckled at his own joke.

"Getting a good night's sleep helped."

She squeezed her fingers around Keir's, silently thanking him for the gift of serenity he'd given her last night. Being held so securely in his arms, surrounded by his heat, was the only thing that had allowed her to drop her guard, shut off her brain and finally relax enough to sleep. The rest had been healing and rejuvenating for her spirit and energy, although waking up with a firm arousal wedged against her thigh and a warm hand cupped possessively over the curve of her bottom had stirred up a very different sort of energy inside her—one that still hummed with a sensual awareness of the man holding her hand.

As tender, protective and compassionate as he'd been with her over the past two days, she suspected that Keir Watson would be a skilled and generous lover. And she'd been half tempted to run her fingers over all that warm, firm skin that stretched tautly over his shoulders and chest, and initiate a kiss to test her theory about just how good they could be together. But when he'd caught her staring her fill of his interestingly handsome face, Keir caught her hips between his hands and lifted her away from the evidence of his desire to set her on the cushions beside him. "Sorry about that. Not exactly stellar timing for that sort of thing, is it?"

His blue eyes danced with a rakish twinkle and her addled, wishful brain heard, *"Oh, what I couldn't do with you for a couple of hours."*

But her ears heard an imminently more practical "Ready to get to work?" before he caught her lips in a good-morning kiss. Then he was standing up, searching the kitchen for fresh coffee and telling her to shower and get dressed while he dug up something for brunch.

As she watched the numbers above the elevator door light up with each floor, Kenna wondered if she'd ever be able to look at a progression of numerals without this wary jump in her pulse again. Or maybe it was the spicy scent of the detective beside her who was making her heart beat a little faster. Had she ever been this attracted to a man before the attack? There were no photographs of any man other than her father on display at the house, no silly little mementos tucked away in any well-organized drawer that could be a sentimental souvenir and certainly no engagement ring box or heart-shaped pendant to indicate evidence of a serious relationship.

Even with amnesia blanking names and faces, wouldn't she remember feeling this deliciously sexy awareness if she'd ever experienced it before? This soul-mate sensation of meeting a personality of equal drive, wit and intelligence? This feeling of being in love?

Love?

The elevator stopped with an abrupt jolt on the fifth floor. Or maybe that jolt was her brain admitting the word *love* and mulling over the possibility of what, exactly, she felt for the detective standing beside her. Kenna pulled her hand from Keir's and hugged her arms around her middle. Gratitude? Certainly. Attraction? Couldn't help herself. But love? How could a mature, sensible woman fall in love in the space of a couple of days?

The obvious answer was that she'd crashed her brain against a brick wall and wasn't thinking sensibly. The less obvious answer was that she was confusing love with something else. And though she wasn't naive enough to think that Keir didn't find her equally attractive, having an overly developed sense of responsibility for a victim and wanting to share a roll on the couch didn't mean he was getting a relationship kind of serious feeling about her, too.

The elevator opened across from a bank of glass doors with a Kleinschmidt, Drexler, Parker and Bond logo plaque up on the wall behind the receptionist's counter inside. Maybe Hellie saw the fact that she'd released Keir's hand as an opening to get a little more personal with her. He unlocked the door and, palming the small of her back, led her across the plush gray carpet to the tall white counter. He hooked his dripping umbrella over the edge of the reception counter and shrugged off his tan raincoat. "Do you remember where your office is?"

Kenna took a moment to look around. Familiar images started to drop into place—the neutral color scheme of the centrally located reception area, the long hallways leading in opposite directions. "Partners' offices are to the left—paralegals and storage rooms to the right." She pointed to the left. "I'm down there."

Hellie took her arm. "Come this way first."

Although Keir used a few extra seconds to scan both hallways, he quickly followed her and Hellie around the counter through the door marked Boardroom. The long room looked the way she remembered from that past board meeting. The heavy walnut table and leather rolling chairs looked familiar, as did the bookshelves and a bar sink complete with coffee cups and liquor glasses. Kenna walked to the row of windows looking out over the city street. Rivulets of rain streaked the tinted glass, giving the buildings across the street and the cars below a gray, gloomy look in the middle of the afternoon. There must be some kind of convention going on at Bartle Hall or a matinee concert at the Folly Theater nearby to account for the bumper-to-bumper parking along each sidewalk and the row of cars lining up to pull into the parking garage kitty-corner from the building.

"Here you are." Kenna turned past Keir unzipping his jacket in the doorway to Hellie pulling something from the safe he'd opened at the far end of the room. He jingled a ring of keys in his hand, and Kenna moved away from the windows to retrieve them. "Arthur ordered spare sets made to award the newbies when they make junior partner. I don't think he'd mind if you kept these until you can get all your keys replaced. What about your car keys—will you be able to get around?"

"I had a spare set at home." She'd found keys for the house, too, that she could use if the security codes didn't work, or she forgot the numbers, and had given a set to Keir.

Hellie pressed the keys into her hand, folding her fingers around them and holding on until she lifted her questioning gaze to his. "What about replacing your driver's license and other cards that were in your purse?"

"I've already called and put a stop on my credit cards. Replacements are in the mail, and I'll be visiting the DMV tomorrow to get my license replaced."

One bushy eyebrow climbed higher on his forehead as he leaned in to whisper, "With Detective Watson?"

Kenna pulled her hand away and glanced over at Keir, who hadn't missed a word of her conversation with Hellie. "I don't know," she answered honestly, remembering Keir's promise to keep her safe until her attacker was found. Although she longed to believe he'd stay with her indefinitely, realistically she knew the man had to return to work. And she doubted she'd be a welcome addition hanging out with his team at precinct headquarters. She was going to have to hire a bodyguard or learn how to face the frightening blanks of her life on her own. Neither option could quell the sudden discomfort that tightened her chest.

"I'd be happy to take you," Hellie offered. He cupped his hands over her shoulders, and she had the feeling he was offering more than a ride to the DMV. "Just say the word and I'm yours."

Not gonna happen. Pasting a smile on her face, Kenna shrugged off his touch and headed for the door. "I'll let you know. Right now I need to track down some information for the police. Thanks again for your help, Hellie."

"Please tell me I don't have to like that guy," Keir said a few moments later as he draped his jacket on the back of a chair over an air vent in Kenna's office while she sat down at her desk and reacquainted herself with her work space.

"I'm pretty sure I don't like him," Kenna admitted, booting up her desktop computer. "I have a feeling I merely tolerate him because he was a friend of my father's—and we have to work together. Those eyebrows of his are a little scary. They remind me of two—"

"Fuzzy caterpillars?"

Kenna laughed, and the tension she'd been feeling, analyzing her feelings for him and thinking about how lost she was going to feel when they had to go their separate ways, receded to a manageable level that she could ignore. Meanwhile, she opened drawers until she found an address book. Keir stood and looked over her shoulder while she thumbed through the pages for the *W*'s. Finally. *Barbara Jean Webster. Hulston Hall.* "That's at a law school." A loud, energetic laugh echoed through her memories and Kenna snapped her fingers. "She's an old friend of mine. We went through law school together."

Keir pulled his notepad from the back pocket of his jeans and perched his hip on the corner of the desk. "Call her. Put it on speaker."

Kenna dialed the number and waited for her friend to answer. "Barbara Jean?"

"Hey, Kenna." Barbara Jean sounded breathless, as if she was in the middle of a workout. "It's good to hear your voice. I heard that you got mugged Friday night. I didn't know if you were up for visitors or I'd have stopped by."

"You heard I was attacked? It wasn't in the news."

Barbara Jean shouted a boy's name and something about tracking mud through the house before she returned to the phone. "The legal community is a small world. I heard it from a friend of a friend. Don't know the details, of course. How are you feeling?"

Kenna could remember dark hair now, and two equally dark-haired children, as she began to place her friend in her life. "I'm a little beat up around the edges."

"I hope the police catch the creep."

"Well, that's the reason I'm calling." Although she still couldn't recall her friend's face, the fast-talking, bighearted personality was feeling more and more familiar. "The police are investigating, and I'm a little foggy on the details leading up to the assault. Can you remind me why we were meeting and where?"

"Honey, are you okay?"

"I will be if you can answer a few questions."

Barbara Jean seemed to be wrestling galoshes off children's feet, but she didn't hesitate to respond. "We were meeting for coffee after you wrapped things up at the courthouse. As to why? You tell me. I was hoping maybe you were coming to me to finally file a sexual harassment lawsuit against your buddy Hellie. Boy, does that man have a problem with keeping his hands to himself! I felt like I had to shower off after that New Year's Eve party at the Drexlers'. It didn't make any difference telling him I had a husband."

"Did I mention a lawsuit?"

"No. Mostly you vented about dealing with too much stress and living under a microscope with Mr. Kleinschmidt dangling that promotion in front of you—how everyone at the firm was scrutinizing your work on the Colbern case."

The squeal of children's voices startled Kenna but quickly faded into silence as Barbara Jean sent them out to the kitchen for snacks.

"You know, when I heard about the mugging, my first thought was that Hellie had done something to you. I wouldn't put it past him if it meant getting you out of the running for senior partner. The man's an idiot. Of course, you made that police detective look like an idiot, too."

Kenna shot Keir an apologetic look. But if he'd gotten a new dent on his ego, he didn't show it. Instead, he gestured for her to keep asking questions and went back to jotting his notes. "And we had coffee at…?"

"Balthazar's."

Keir jotted a message on his notepad and showed it to her. *When did you leave Balthazar's?*

"Hey, do you remember about what time I left the coffee shop?"

Barbara Jean sounded as if she'd finally caught her breath. "That's an odd question."

"I couldn't remember the exact time." She couldn't remember meeting her friend at all. But she could recall sharing an apartment with Barbara Jean in Columbia, Missouri—and making coffee and red licorice runs when they'd been up late studying for exams. "The detective here says it could help if I retrace my steps leading up to the attack."

"Let's see. You left Balthazar's at almost straight-up three o'clock. I had to get home to meet the kids when the bus dropped them off after school—and you said you had a five o'clock, and you were going home to get changed."

"I went home?"

Where she'd fought with someone and clobbered her head on the patio wall.

"That's what you told me."

"Did I say who I was meeting?"

"No. But I gather it was a man. Why else would you go home to get gussied up? Although you were already wearing one of your power suits and a pair of those knock-'em-dead high heels." Barbara Jean hissed an apologetic sigh. "Sorry. Poor choice of words."

A *"Don't worry"* died on her lips when the significance of what her friend had said registered. Kenna leaned toward the phone. "Do you remember what suit I was wearing? What heels?"

"The police want to know what you wore to coffee with me?"

"It could be important."

"Um, let's see. Oh, sure. It was your kick-ass-in-court suit—the tan Armani—and the Jimmy Choos you splurged on down on the Plaza." Barbara Jean scoffed. "You know, the ones with the mile-high heels? Like you need to be any taller."

Kenna remembered her clothes being bagged up in the hospital several hours after the assault. She reached over to squeeze Keir's knee. "I never changed my clothes. That's what I was wearing when I was attacked."

Keir nodded. "That narrows the timeline considerably."

"Between three and five o'clock."

"What's that?" Barbara Jean asked, thinking Kenna had been talking to her.

Keir scrawled a question on his notepad and she read the message. *Rose petals?*

"Barbara Jean? This will sound strange, too, but…" Keir's hand settled over hers where it fisted on the desk. She turned her palm up to meet his. She could do this. "Did I mention anything about roses? Or about someone stalking me?"

Barbara Jean gasped. "Oh, honey. Is that what happened to you? No. I wish I'd known. Maybe I could have helped. You just said you needed to get away and have a normal conversation with someone you could trust. You did seem to be wound up pretty tight. I figured it was the stress of the trial, but I guess this stalker creep was weighing on your mind. Knowing you, you probably thought you could handle the situation yourself. You should have said something."

Keir closed his notepad, indicating he'd gotten the information he needed. "Thanks, Barbara Jean. I appreciate the help."

"Anytime, my friend. And hey, whenever you want to leave the good ol' boys' network and go into a partnership with Walter and me, just say the word. We'll take good care of you. I know you're loyal to Kleinschmidt, Drexler because your dad was a founding partner, but if the old guy promotes Hellie ahead of you, I'd jump ship."

"I'll think about it. Thanks." Kenna disconnected the call with a wistful smile. So there were two people in this world she trusted without question. Barbara Jean Webster and the man sitting beside her, who maybe didn't have much reason to trust *her*.

She pulled her hand from beneath Keir's. "Still dislike Hellie?" She tried to make the question sound like a teasing gibe, but the reality of her getting Colbern acquitted at Keir's expense made the joke fall flat. "If Arthur had assigned him instead of me, you might have won your case."

He stood and pulled her to her feet beside him. "Don't you go soft on me now, Counselor. You beat me, fair and square. I didn't like it. I still don't. But that just means that next time I appear in court, I'm going to up my game and put together a case that not even the great Kenna Parker can tear apart."

She arched an eyebrow and tilted her skeptical gaze to his. "The great Kenna Parker?"

"Too much?"

She squeezed her thumb and forefinger together and smiled. "Li'l bit."

He traced the curve of her lip with his fingertip. "That's better. Besides, friend or foe, I'd rather look at your legs than Hellie's bushy eyebrows any day."

Although her lip still tingled from the touch of Keir's finger, she knew they were here for business, not flirty reassurances. She nodded toward the phone. "Chatting with Barbara Jean helped. I never got the chance to change my clothes that night. I never made my five o'clock."

"I think you did."

Of course. "Whoever I had that appointment with—"

"Is the man who tried to kill you."

The stitches at the base of her skull throbbed with the dire realization. "That's why no one called to see why I never showed up for dinner." She pointed to the appointment calendar she'd pulled up on her computer screen. Except for the court appearance in the morning, and the initials *B.J.* at three o'clock, the square for Friday was blank. "Why didn't I write down who I was meeting? Clearly, it wasn't work related or my assistant would have posted it."

"Maybe that's exactly what the meeting was about—work." Kenna frowned, needing more of an explanation. "I just heard your friend rattle off a lot of complaints about Helmut Bond. Sexual harassment? Good ol' boys' network? Vying for the same promotion? If he sees you as a threat—that's motive. Being a longtime family friend, you'd be comfortable inviting him to your house. You'd probably try to reason out the conflict with him before you took any kind of legal action." Keir shrugged. "Or maybe you did threaten legal action and that set him off. He's certainly kept an eye on you since the attack. He could be trying to see if you remember him being there."

Personal aversions aside, Kenna hated to think that someone her father had mentored could get angry enough to hurt her like this. There had to be another answer. "What about the phone calls and letters? All that happened before the attack—before I would have confronted Hellie. Those are detailed, planned actions, meant to frighten and intimidate me." She swept her hand in front of her face. "This is impulse, not a patient, calculated terror campaign. Helmut Bond is glib and annoying, not violent."

"Unless something you said or did at that meeting triggered the rage he's been holding in check."

Kenna overlapped the front edges of the cotton cardigan she wore, hugging herself against the chill that shivered through her body. "Then we've still got a lousy case, Detective. I have no idea what I said or did, much less who I said or did it to."

Keir rubbed his hands up and down her arms, trying to instill in her the warmth and confidence she couldn't find. His voice was a hushed, intimate whisper of encouragement. "If you won't consider your buddy Bond, then we'll go find more suspects. If we can't have eyewitness testimonies, then let's dig up all the circumstantial evidence we can find and put together a list of persons of interest who might have motive to hurt you."

Kenna knew what he was asking. "The BED file. Brian Elliott. The Rose Red Rapist."

Keir crossed to the door and opened it. "We know he didn't send the letters with the rose petals, because they'd be marked with a prison stamp. And he didn't make those calls, because the prison would have a record of them."

"And he couldn't be the man in the hoodie watching me, because he's locked up in Jefferson City."

"But he could easily hire someone to do the work for him."

Steeling her shoulders on a resigned breath, Kenna grabbed her keys and moved into the hallway ahead of him, preceding him down the long hallway to the file storage room. "Technically, he's still my client, so I won't be able to show you the file."

"Are any of the contacts, victims or witnesses in his file your clients?"

"No."

"I've got that list of everybody who's visited Elliott in the past three months. While you're reading files, I'll start making phone calls. All I need are names, and then I can do the legwork to check alibis and criminal histories and find out who has a grudge against you."

Kenna was sorely afraid of just how long that list might be.

Nearly half an hour later, Kenna was hugging an armload of file folders to her chest when she and Keir left the storage room. "I feel like I'm back in law school," she said, waiting for Keir to lock the door behind him before heading to the boardroom, where they could spread out at the conference table. "Toting around case files I have to memorize for Professor Owenson's class."

"Are you sure you don't want me to carry those for you?"

"It's a conflict of interest for a police officer—"

"What's he doing here?" Kenna stopped short when the compact, blond-haired man who'd been conversing with Hellie at the reception counter charged down the hallway to meet her. The accusing finger he'd pointed at Keir swung toward her. "Conspiring with the enemy?"

The man was middle-aged, angry and completely unfamiliar to her. "Excuse me?"

"Kenna?" Keir stepped up beside her to make the introduction. "This is Andrew Colbern."

Shock drew her back half a step as she sorted through her memories for an earlier consultation that would make the sneering expression spark a recognition in her. She looked over at Keir, knowing this man's trial was a point of conflict between them. But the only hint that this unexpected meeting might have poked that sore point was for Keir to shift his posture, splaying his fingers at his waist, possibly reminding the other man that he wore a gun, or maybe just relaxing his stance to show the other man he wasn't intimidated by him.

"There's no way he's attending this meeting," Colbern announced, either uncaring or unaware of Keir subtly nudging his shoulder in front of Kenna. "He's the cop who tricked me into saying I wanted to have Devon killed."

Hellie placed a hand on Colbern's arm. "Andrew, as your attorney, I advise you not to say anything in front of Detective Watson."

Kenna was having a hard time getting up to speed on this conversation. But she knew a manipulation when she saw one. She looked past Dr. Colbern to Hellie. "You set up this meeting as soon as I hung up after asking you to let me into the office. You know I'm not ready to deal with clients."

"Somebody better be," Colbern warned. "I want to know what you're going to do to get this stain off my reputation. Do you know how many of my patients have canceled appointments since I was arrested? Devon has a lot of social contacts, and I know that witch is spreading lies about me."

Keir's voice remained calm. "You're talking about a PR campaign, Colbern, not legal action. That's not Ms. Parker's area of expertise."

"Why are you even talking to me, Watson? How is this any of your business?"

"Kenna Parker is my business."

Colbern's blue-eyed gaze darted between Kenna and Keir. "Oh, so it's like that, is it?"

"Dr. Colbern is *our* client," Hellie emphasized, steering the conversation away from Keir. "I wanted to reassure him that we're ready to move forward to block his wife's civil suit."

"But we're not. *I'm* not," Kenna reminded him.

"But we will be," Hellie insisted. His brown eyes narrowed with a silent message she didn't care to read. "I have a plan of action mapped out. I just need you to confer—add your two cents, as it were."

"Two cents? Ha." Andrew Colbern's snort was filled with bitterness. "With what this firm is costing me, I ought to be getting a lot more advice than that."

Kenna wasn't sure if her gut was telling her to

be leery of Dr. Colbern or Hellie. But she knew she didn't want to deal with either man's attitude right now. "I'm sorry, gentlemen." She lifted the files she carried. "But I'm in the middle of a project. Doctor, why don't you call my assistant tomorrow and make an appointment for later in the week?"

"Don't bother, Andrew."

Kenna read the flush of temper brewing beneath Hellie's tan cheeks.

"I have my car downstairs. What do you say to an early dinner, and you and I can discuss your wife's threats there?"

"Let's just reschedule when Kenna's available." The doctor shook his head, eyeing Keir. "I may not like the company she keeps, but I think we need her input on how we're going to move forward against Devon. This afternoon was a waste of my time."

"Very well." Hellie fixed that bright white smile on his face, but the door was already closing on Andrew Colbern's emphatic exit. "I'll call you."

Kenna was suddenly very tired. Maybe she'd overtaxed her energy level too soon after being in the hospital. And maybe this was the kind of stress she'd wanted to talk to Barbara Jean about. Perhaps she did need to consider her friend's offer to work for a smaller firm.

"How dare you embarrass me like that in front of a client?" Hellie seized Kenna by the shoulders, shaking loose two of the folders she carried. "Bringing your boy toy to work—"

"Hey, pal." Keir snatched Hellie by the wrist and twisted his arm behind his back, earning a grunt of pain as he pulled him away from Kenna. "You don't threaten the lady."

Surprised by both Hellie's outburst and Keir's swift response, Kenna stooped down to retrieve the folders from the floor. "It was presumptuous of you to arrange a meeting without informing me, Hellie. Are you so worried you can't win a case without me on the team? Or that you're going to lose a client?"

"I'm not worried about anything." Hellie shrugged off Keir's hold as soon as the younger man loosened his grip. "Except maybe your choice in men." He grabbed his umbrella and raincoat off the reception counter where he'd left a puddle of water on the carpet beneath and strode toward the door. "I thought I knew you, that I could count on you the way I counted on your father. But you've changed. Don't call me for any more favors until you've come to your senses."

Once the elevator door had closed behind Hellie, Keir turned back to Kenna. "Do you still believe that conniver couldn't snap and lose his temper?"

Chapter Nine

Kenna's growling stomach startled her awake. Her chin slipped off her hand and she was painfully aware of the throbbing in her wrist after bending it back at the unnatural angle to support her head. It took a few seconds to orient herself to her surroundings. Folders and paperwork stacked in various piles across the long conference table. Rain pattering at the window. Grinning man watching her from the end of the table.

"Please tell me I wasn't drooling."

Keir set down his phone and the ink pen he'd been using. "Nothing significant."

She tossed a wad of paper at him. "Very funny."

He caught it and tossed it right back before checking the time. "We've been at this for three hours, and Dr. McBride said you should take it easy for a while. Ready to call it a day?"

"Did we find any viable suspects?"

"A few." He picked up the legal pad he'd borrowed

to record notes from the phone calls he'd made and thumbed through several pages of yellow paper to reveal all the names he'd been able to cross off from the lists they'd generated. "Between Hud and me and my sister, Liv, we're narrowing it down. The women Brian Elliott preyed on whom we've been able to reach thus far have solid alibis for three to five p.m. on Friday, so we can rule them out as your attacker."

"Do you really think a woman could do this to me?"

"If she subdued you somehow—drugged you, or a blitz attack. We shouldn't automatically rule out the possibility." He read the first names on the page where he'd stopped. "April King. She was working her shift at Truman Medical Center." He picked up the pen and scratched through her name. "Tabitha and Ezekiel Rule—the victim and her husband—were involved in a fender bender out near Lenexa. State Patrol has them on the scene for several hours." He scratched those names out, too. "Genie D'Angelo—committed suicide two years after Elliott sexually assaulted her."

"How horrible." When he scratched out the last young woman's name, Kenna's heart twisted with guilt. It was difficult to uphold the law and ensure due process for everyone when faced with a loss like that. "What about the family members or friends who blame me for defending the man who hurt their loved ones? Does anyone stand out there?"

"That's a bigger list. But we'll keep hitting the Rose Red Rapist angle, since you seemed suspicious of Brian Elliott before your amnesia." Keir flipped the legal pad back to its first page and stood. "By the way, I went with my gut and checked out Hellie Bond's alibi. He was more than happy to tell me how wrong I am. But it's sketchy at best. He claims he went for a drive in the country. Alone. Said his girl left town and he was missing her."

"You're so determined it's him." Kenna rolled her chair away from the table and pushed to her feet. Could someone she saw nearly every day of her life, someone her father had trusted, someone who claimed he cared for her, really be so insecure or vindictive that he'd spend months trying to drive her crazy or leave her scarred for life? "I would have thought Andrew Colbern resented me more than Hellie ever could. Until today. Maybe he does have motive to send me rose petals to remind me of my biggest and most unpopular case—to make me paranoid and second-guess every choice I make— to put me off my game just when Arthur is about to name one of us senior partner." She picked up one of the files and straightened the papers before closing it. "Maybe there's someone in every file here who wants me to crack up or bow out of the human race or simply fail at getting the things I want."

Keir placed his hand on top of the folders Kenna

was stacking to return to the storage room. "Do you want to be a senior partner?"

Kenna honestly didn't know the answer to that question anymore. "I thought I was breaking through some kind of glass ceiling, making a statement for women, and I was proud of that. I felt I deserved the promotion and worked hard to bring in big-money clients. I wanted it because that's what my father always envisioned for me, and I loved the idea of honoring his legacy."

"If you want it, go for it. And don't let Helmut Bond or whoever this bastard is stop you from being who you want to be. He's one man, and he doesn't get to win. If your dream changes and you want something else, you'll be a success at that, too, because that's who you are. The Kenna I've gotten to know doesn't settle for halfway or second best. I can't imagine any father not being proud of that legacy." He gestured to the remaining folders strewn across the table. "And don't forget that there are good people in these files you've helped, too. Maybe their names don't make headlines like a billionaire with a sexual depravity. But they're there. Innocent people who needed a champion to represent them. Not everybody in these files wants to hurt you. You may have more friends out there than you think."

Heartened by the rallying show of support, empowered in a way that only this man seemed to manage, Kenna threw her arms around Keir's neck and hugged him tight. She turned her lips to the collar of his white button-down shirt and kissed the warm beat of his pulse. "Thank you."

He wrapped his arms around her, pulling her into his ample heat and sealing the embrace.

"I don't know if you're always like this, or if you're only like this with me at this moment, but you said what I needed to hear. I think that I'm a strong woman. But you make me stronger. Be sure to add that to the list of things I owe you for."

Kenna kissed the corner of his firm mouth. With an eager moan, Keir curved his mouth over hers to accept and deepen the invitation. Sliding her fingers into his hair, Kenna had every intention of taking up where every other potent kiss between them had left off. But another noisy grumble in her stomach vibrated between them. With a sound that was half laugh and half sigh of regret, Keir pulled his lips from hers. He rested his forehead against hers and looked down into her eyes. "One day, woman, we're going to finish this."

His voice was raw and deep, and the promise behind it left her embarrassingly weak in the knees. "I'm going to hold you to that promise."

He pressed a warm, ticklish kiss to the end of her nose, then pulled away entirely. "In the meantime, I'd better feed you."

"Are you going to treat me to some of Millie's cooking again?"

Keir pulled his jacket off the back of his chair and shrugged into it. "I'd be just as happy to go to your place and heat up that leftover casserole."

"Why don't we swing past Balthazar's and get a couple of cups of java to go on the way?" she suggested. "We could ask a few questions of any staff or customers who might have seen someone following me Friday afternoon."

"You're relentless. Did anyone ever tell you you'd make one heck of a cop?"

"Never."

He laughed out loud and that made her smile. This man made her feel like teasing and laughing and smiling again, instead of hiding in her big, empty house and maintaining rigid control over every aspect of her life.

"All right. Balthazar's it is." He kissed her temple, then circled around the table and out the door. "Gather up what you need. We can read through the rest of these at the house. I'll go bring the car around so you don't get soaked. Lock up and meet me down at the front door."

Moving with a lighter step than she had had all day, Kenna quickly gathered up the folders that were ready to be refiled and locked them in the storage room. She grabbed a tote bag from her office closet and hurried back to the boardroom to pack Keir's notes and the remaining case files.

As she was closing one of the files she'd kept on

her defense of Austin Meade—a former crime boss's nephew, who'd been more of an embarrassment than a success in the defunct family business—a sheet of white paper caught her eye. It wasn't a transcript of a deposition or a handwritten note. It wasn't a photograph. A little tremor of apprehension shivered through her as she reached for the blank page and pulled it out. If there was one rose petal… Only, it wasn't a plain sheet of paper, after all. Kenna's relief blossomed into curiosity when she saw the small pencil drawing of a geometric figure, hastily drawn in the top left corner.

She remembered this image.

But how? From where?

Although it was basically a rectangular shape, the edges were scalloped and there were several caret-shaped marks drawn in the blank space around the design inside the rectangle. Two lines swooshed toward a small circle that sat off-center, and was surrounded by eight points of a star. "It's a spur. A spur off a cowboy boot."

She didn't know any cowboys, did she? What did the symbol mean?

Knowing that Keir would be coming for her soon, she went to the bank of windows to look out. Groups of people were hurrying down the sidewalk, and traffic was backing up in the street. The event at Bartle Hall or one of the theaters must have let out. And with the rain still coming down and people eager to get into dry cars and go home, no one seemed particularly anxious to let anyone else merge into traffic. She wanted to show the drawing to Keir. She wanted to see if it struck a familiar chord with him, too. But she couldn't see the black Charger anywhere. He probably had to drive around the block to get to the front of the building.

Eager to show him her discovery, Kenna locked up the offices and rode the elevator down to the first floor. She waited inside the lobby doors, amused by the people hurrying by with their raincoats and umbrellas, and those without protection from the elements hurrying by even faster. She was keeping one eye out for Keir and mentally scanning through her Swiss cheese brain for the significance of the spur to fall into place when she gradually became aware that not everyone was rushing through the rain.

There was one person standing perfectly still. One person watching. Watching her.

Her heart beating a stitch faster, her chest expanding and contracting with quicker breaths, she scanned both sides of the street, up and down the block, until she zeroed in on the absence of movement. There. Lurking in the shadows at the entrance to the parking garage across the street.

The faceless man in the black hoodie.

Her lips parted to take a deeper breath as an urgent sense of being singled out for some evil purpose fluttered through her pulse. Kenna recoiled a step from the shadowed face that was still there each time a pedestrian walked past or a car drove by. She was afraid. She was so damn tired of being afraid. She needed to make it stop.

He doesn't get to win.

Keir's vehement words resonated in her head, tamping down the fear. All this guy did was show up where she was, and watch. She'd seen him twice now. And he'd probably been there a third time when Keir spotted him near the alley where he'd found her. Maybe Hoodie Guy had followed her more often and she just hadn't noticed. His strength was in the shadows, in his anonymity. Well, she could take that advantage away with one simple task. She was a strong woman. She took action. She wasn't giving this faceless stranger the chance to terrorize her again.

"I think it's time the two of us meet." And this time, she wouldn't forget his face.

Looping the tote bag over her neck and shoulder, Kenna pushed open the door and stepped outside. Rain slapped her in the face and she squinted her eyes against the onslaught. The guy wasn't moving. Maybe she could use the crowd and traffic to her advantage and get close enough to see beneath the hood before he realized she was there. That was all she had to do. She didn't have to confront him. She just needed to see his face.

When a group of schoolchildren and parents jostled past, she turned and walked with them, ducking behind a parked van as soon as she reached it. She peeked around the taillight of the van and saw Hoodie Guy slowly moving his head back and forth. Good. He'd lost sight of her. For once, she had the advantage.

When he turned his scan away from her, she darted between stopped and slow-moving cars until she reached his side of the street. Blending in was a little trickier here, since she was moving against the flow of pedestrians leaving the theater in the next block. Just a little closer. *Look this direction.* Kenna reached the entrance to the garage and paused. The rain had soaked through her hair and was running down her scalp and beading in her eyelashes. He was on the other side of this concrete archway, just a few yards away. She'd never be closer to the truth.

But the fear was sinking its talons into her again. She should have thought this through better. She should have waited for Keir. She should get her stupid cell phone replaced so she could call her protector and tell him what she was doing. But what if Hoodie Guy was on the move and she lost him? What if he was already gone?

"Just count to three and poke your head around the corner," she murmured, steeling her resolve. "That's all you have to do. One. Two."

"Looking for me, Kenna?"

She heard the toneless whisper the same moment a gloved hand closed around her shoulder and she screamed a startled yelp and jerked away from his grasp. Kenna spun around the concrete arch to face him. "Where…?"

She heard breathless laughter. Heavy boots on concrete.

"Ma'am?" She yelped a second time at the touch of another hand on the wet sleeve of her sweater. But this time she looked up into the apologetic face of a tall, lanky cowboy. "Sorry. Are you all right?"

A Good Samaritan. Not the terror that lived in the fringes of her mind every single day of her life. "Do you have a phone on you?"

"Sure do." Water ran off the brim of his hat when he nodded. He pulled a cell phone from a pocket inside his corduroy jacket.

"I need you to call the police." The sound of heavy footsteps was fading. Hoodie Guy was getting away. Again. "There's a man following me. He just accosted me. Black hoodie. Ski mask. Blue jeans. Give them this address."

"Okay. Do you want to wait with my wife…? Ma'am?"

Kenna hoped the cowboy took directions well, because she wasn't coming back to repeat them. She ran all the way up the ramp to the next half level where she could hear the garage's metal infrastructure ringing with the heavy tromp of the man's thick-soled boots. She was slightly breathless herself by the time she spotted him at the far end, running with a bit of a limp down the center of the aisle. She crouched near the trunks of cars as she gave chase. "Hey, you! Why are you following me?"

He disappeared up the ramp to the next floor. Ignoring the burning in her lungs, she ran to the base of the ramp. She saw his torso, legs and work boots though the crisscrossed steel railings attached to the open interior edge of each parking level. Still no face.

"Did you do this to me?" No answer. "What do you want? How did I ever hurt you? Why don't you talk to me like a man would?"

Kenna raced toward the ramp until she realized he'd stopped running. Through the railing she saw him brace his gloved hands on his knees and lean forward as a deep cough shook his body and he fought to catch his breath. Creeping back toward his position on the half level below him, Kenna moved toward the railing, thinking she could peer up between the bars and get a look at his face. If he'd turn just a fraction of an inch, she could finally fill one empty spot in her memory. She panted through her open mouth, breathing silently, hiding her approach. He was holding his side now, his breath wheezing like rales in his chest. Was the man older? Injured? Out of shape? All three?

Then he seemed to catch his breath and hold it as he turned. Kenna watched the hood, waiting for his face to appear. She was so crushed to see the ski mask hiding his features that she nearly missed his hand coming around at the same time. But a glint of the garage's yellowish lights reflected off a long steel blade. He laughed as he thrust the knife toward her and slashed it through the air. Once. Twice. Thrice as he mimicked slashing her throat.

Kenna jerked back as if the blade had actually cut her.

Her hands flew to her neck and the man laughed until another coughing fit took hold. "Oh, yeah," he rasped. "Now you're scared. That's how I like it."

In the moment she blinked, he'd vanished around the next concrete post. She heard a horn honking and a screech of tires spinning over pavement in the distance. "Kenna!"

Red-and-blue lights flashed in her peripheral vision as she ran to the railing and shook the metal like the bars of a jail cell. "You coward! I'm going to rip that mask right off your face! Talk to me!"

Was that why she'd blanked out any memory of her attacker's face? Because there'd been no face for her to remember?

"Kenna!"

The swirling lights were blinding now as her eyes filled with tears of emotional exhaustion. A car slammed on its brakes and skidded to a halt behind her. The man was long gone. So was her hope. There were only two ways this whole nightmare was going to end. Either she'd have some kind of nervous breakdown or she'd be dead.

"You single-minded, stubborn…"

Kenna was still clinging to the railing with a white-knuckled grip when Keir ran up behind her.

"Are you hurt?"

She shook her head. The man in the hoodie hadn't harmed her, not physically, at least.

She was aware of how heavy her clothes were with the rain and how she squished the puddles inside her tennis shoes when she wiggled her toes. She was aware of Keir's hands cupping either side of her neck, then sliding up and down her arms. Each touch was an urgent brand that warmed her, then quickly dissipated and left a chill in its place when he pulled away.

"Woman, you're like ice."

Kenna stared at the drops of water dripping from his dark hair onto his white shirt as he shrugged off his jacket and wrapped it around her shoulders.

"What were you thinking? *I* chase the bad guys. *You* defend them."

Wow. That was a painfully awkward reminder of what her life had distilled down to these past few days. She pushed from his grasp, swiping away the tears before too many of them spilled over.

"Ah, hell, baby, I'm sorry. I wasn't thinking." He caught a tear with the pad of his thumb and flicked it away before pulling her into his arms. "You scared me. I saw you take off after that perp by yourself, getting farther and farther away from me. And all the damn traffic—I couldn't get through until I put up my siren."

Keir was as soaked to the skin as she was, but his body exuded a warmth and vitality she couldn't seem to generate.

"Didn't you see the knife? He got you alone once before and look at what he did to you. Look how he hurt you. I can't let him hurt you again." He leaned back to pinch her chin between his thumb and forefinger and tilt her face up to his. "I need you to say something right now or I'm taking you to the hospital."

Kenna braced her palm against his chest, seeking the solid beat of his heart and willing hers to answer with that same kind of strength. "I was thinking I could put an end to this nightmare if I could see his face. I thought it would help me remember."

By now there were other red-and-blue lights filling the parking garage like the thick mist hanging in the air. Keir walked her around the front of his car, waving aside offers from uniformed officers to call for an ambulance and directing them to post a search perimeter to find any trace of the man who'd threatened her. "Did you see him? Did you remember anything?"

A long, thin knife blade slashing at her face. But nothing useful.

"He wore a mask. And he hates me. He enjoys doing this to me."

Keir muttered a curse and opened the passenger side door. "Get in the car. You're wet clean through. The last thing I need is for you to get sick."

Kenna tightened her grip on his shirt. She didn't want to move. She didn't want to lose contact with him.

"Please, babe." He shook his head. "I mean Counselor. Kenna." He'd go back to calling her Ms. Parker or the Terminator if she didn't get into the car in the next few seconds.

Right. He needed her to be strong, too. She could dig down deep and find a way to keep it together for him.

"I'll be okay, Keir." She sat on the edge of the seat, facing him, still holding on to that fistful of his shirt, and prayed it was a promise she could keep. He reached past her to crank the heater up to high, then knelt in front of her, just as he had two nights ago when he rescued her from that alley.

He pried her fingers from the wet cotton and captured both her hands between his, rubbing some warmth into them. "I need to work this, Kenna. I need to leave you for a few minutes, but I have to know you'll be safe. I called Hud and alerted my major crime unit. I've got a whole team of officers here and a citywide BOLO for anyone matching Hoodie Guy's description. But somebody needs to run the show until the senior officer gets here."

"I love that you called in the cavalry for me, but

you won't find him." This guy was too good at blending in. "He probably had a change of clothes stashed somewhere in the garage, or the hoodie and jeans were masking whatever he's wearing now, and he walked out with them in a backpack or briefcase."

"I have a feeling you're right. But I have to try." He threaded his fingers into her wet hair and lifted it away from her face. "You'll have to replace those bandages so your stitches don't get wet."

"I'll take care of it."

He still wasn't convinced it was all right to leave her. She reached out and captured his jaw between her hands and leaned over to kiss him. It was tender, potent, brief. She pulled back a few inches and whispered, "You can call me babe or baby if you want. If it makes you feel better. But only you, and not in front of your friends. Now go. Do your job. You're good at it, you know."

"I'm gonna get this guy, babe."

Nodding, Kenna pulled her legs into the car. Keir waited for her to lock the doors before he strode off to join a group of officers. She watched him direct them to various assignments. They each nodded and moved to do his bidding.

While KCPD worked to get some kind of clue on Hoodie Guy's identity or whereabouts, Kenna needed something else to concentrate on while she waited for answers. But it was hard to put together any kind of strategic plan when her memory was riddled with holes and the evidence that could help her defeat her stalker was practically nonexistent.

But the heaviness of the bag in her lap reminded her she had other cases she could be working on. She pulled the strap of the tote bag off over her head and retrieved the file with the odd drawing. The papers inside were soft with moisture and trying to stick. She carefully pulled them apart and held the pages in front of the vent to dry. She studied the drawing from different angles, certain she'd seen that image before, but not quite able to place it. Maybe if she read more about the case itself, something would click.

Twenty minutes later, when Keir climbed in behind the wheel of his car, she thought she had her answer. But she needed to verify one thing before it became an admissible fact.

"Nothing yet." He turned off his warning lights and pulled the magnetic beacon off the roof of his car. "We think he made it to the south stairwell, changed his clothes somewhere along the way and disappeared into the crowd outside. We found some boot prints on the stairs that could be his, but we found a lot of shoe prints in the gravel and mud there. A good lawyer would argue it's impossible to make a definitive match."

Kenna knew the last comment was a wry joke for her benefit, but her only response was, "I need to see your phone."

Other than a curious narrowing of his eyes, he

didn't question the request. He pulled the phone out of his pocket and handed it to her. "Who's your provider? We can stop at the phone store and have them transfer your contacts to a new device."

"Tomorrow, maybe." She tapped the camera icon and opened his pictures. "I just need to see… Here. At least I can find the answer to something. I think this is a match."

"What's a match?"

"I may not be able to solve my problems, but I think I can help with one of yours." She put the phone in his open palm and held the drawing up beside it. "Look."

"This is Grandpa's shooter. I hardly think your assault is connected."

"No." She reached over to enlarge the image of the man who'd put a bullet in Seamus Watson and pointed to the silver and brass rectangle at the center of the screen. "But this guy *is* connected to one of my case files."

"Son of a…" Keir looked over at Kenna, then back at the two images. He saw the same thing she had seen.

"That drawing was made by a witness in a murder investigation four years ago. A professional hit. He said the killer was wearing a belt buckle that looked like that." She showed him the name on the folder where she'd found the drawing. "The Austin Meade trial. He was up on several charges, including a murder for hire to eliminate the owner of an auto repair business who wouldn't sell the building and land to him."

"KCPD put the Meade family out of business years ago."

"Well, apparently they didn't catch this guy. In Meade's deposition he tried to bargain with some information but couldn't give a name. He said the deal was made by contacting the hit man through an unlisted number and asking for a Gin Rickey."

"Like the drink?"

Kenna nodded. She tucked the paper back in the folder and put it away in the tote bag at her feet. While studying the details of the drawing, she'd had a thought that was as disquieting as not knowing the identity of her faceless attacker. "Do the notch marks on the buckle mean what I think they do?"

"Probably." Keir's tone was grim. "The number of jobs he's completed."

"I know it not a complete answer, but—"

"It gives me something to go on. I can look up similar incidents, maybe even talk to Meade in prison." He swiped the picture away and pulled up his contacts to text a message to his father and brothers. "I'll let them know we might have a break in the case."

"There's a general physical description of him in the file, too. I'll type it up for you and include it with a copy of the drawing. It looks like a unique work of art, not something that was mass-produced. You could track down artists and retailers who might sell metalwork like that, too."

Keir sent his messages and set his phone in the console between them. He reached across to capture her hand and pull it to his lips for a kiss. "Thank you."

Kenna knew right then that the two of them would never be enemies again. It gladdened her heart to the point of bursting and warmed the chill from her body. She wasn't a horrible person who defended the bad guys—she helped the good guys, too. And if she believed that forty-eight hours was long enough to really get to know someone—what his deepest needs, fears and beliefs were—and fall in love, she would have admitted that, too.

"YEAH, DAD." KEIR was loading the dishwasher in Kenna's kitchen while he updated his father on the forward movement on the investigation into Seamus's shooting. "Liv is pulling rap sheets on any known hit men in the area. Niall is going through lab records to see if the belt buckle showed up as evidence in any other cases. And before he leaves town, Duff is putting out feelers on the street to see if anyone knows how to contact this Gin Rickey guy now."

"Sounds like you're on top of things. And you informed the detectives officially assigned to the case?"

"Yes, sir." Although, admittedly, that had been an afterthought once he'd gotten word to his family.

He added detergent to the machine and started the wash cycle before taking one more walk around the downstairs to secure the doors and windows before turning in himself.

"And Kenna? How is she doing? Your grandfather asked when she'd be coming by the house again. I think he's sweet on her."

Keir grinned. The old man had good taste. "I sent her upstairs to get some sleep." He checked the back doors and patio outside. Doors locked. Security lights on. The wind was picking up dirt and debris and flinging it against the glass panes as the next wave of thunderstorms rolled in. The overcast sky blotted out any moonlight, shrouding the mansion in darkness and making the hour seem even later than it was. "I'll be heading up myself when we're done. It's been a long day."

"Son. If you love this one, don't let her get away."

"I have to save her first, Dad. Then I'll start thinking about how real these feelings are."

"You know, when I was fresh out of college, fulfilling my ROTC commitment, I was excited about going off to see the world for six years. I was going to sow a lot of wild oats and live a grand adventure until I came back home and went to work for the department."

Keir paused in the foyer at his father's deep sigh.

"My first post was in the UK and I met your mother the second day I was there. I didn't need to be an intelligence officer to know I'd found the one. The third day I told her so and she said she already knew. So much for waiting until the time was right to settle down."

Keir loved hearing these stories about his parents before he was born, but he understood the underlying parental advice being offered, as well. "Dad, I didn't call to talk about my love life."

"I know. Maybe I'm just thinking about your mom tonight. She died on a stormy night like this."

Keir felt a pang of melancholy as he recalled the beautiful woman with the lilting Irish accent.

"You know we lost her way too soon. Makes me glad I didn't waste any time sowin' those oats and not being with her."

"I'm glad you didn't, either."

"Love you, son."

"Love you, too, Dad." Keir disconnected the call and pulled up the tail of his untucked shirt to stuff the phone into his jeans.

He smiled at the memories of his mother playing in the tree house with him, and sitting in her lap as she read him a bedtime story. He grinned as he checked the lock on the front door and peeked through the side windows to make sure the security lights were shining through the trees along the curving driveway down to the gate. He remembered the time-outs alone in his room his mother had given him when he didn't mind her rules. For a social kid, it was a dire punishment for the few minutes it lasted. And to be denied one of his mother's pastries with hand-whipped cream because he'd "borrowed" Liv's dollhouse and painted it with camouflage to be a base for his action figures? Yeah. He missed his mom tonight, too.

Keir shut off the foyer light and headed up the stairs. How many memories had been stolen from Kenna? Although she seemed to have a better recollection of the distant past than of more recent events, she must feel violated to have something as personal as a memory stolen from her.

He reached the landing and turned to see a light shining through Kenna's open door. What aversion did that woman have to sleeping? He wondered if she'd developed a taste for sleeping with a long, warm body nestled against her as quickly as he had last night. Picking up the fresh scent of the citrusy shampoo she used, he knocked and walked into her bedroom. "Kenna?"

He found her inside her closet, staring at the rows of shoes displayed on the shelves of a floor-to-ceiling rack. "What happened to my other shoe?"

She'd showered and was wearing those funny blue pajama pants again. Her damp hair was a shade darker, like sweet latte, and it was making little wet spots above the swell of each breast on her turquoise T-shirt. The marks on her face had been cleaned and were open to the air, highlighting her classic bone structure like badges of honor. She was barefoot like he was, and Keir's heart constricted at the regal beauty that couldn't be compromised by stitches or *Dr. Who* pants.

"Find the shoe, find the man." She stopped counting off sexy heels and running shoes and turned to face him. "He has it, doesn't he—some weird kind of souvenir or trophy like the notches in that killer's belt buckle?"

Keir splayed his hands at his waist, glad he'd untucked his shirt earlier so the long tails masked the way other parts of his body were reacting to her cool brand of smart, sexy strength. "Speaking of belt buckles—that lead you gave me has given my family hope they haven't felt in months." He thought of all the times he'd teased her about tabulating what she owed him. "I'd say we're even now, Counselor."

Kenna turned the light out in the closet and joined him in the room that was now lit only by the lamp beside her four-poster bed. "Not by a long shot."

"I'm the one keeping tabs and I say we're even. The debt is settled. I say thank you, and you say you're welcome." She walked right up to him, stopping close enough that he could dip his head and kiss her without moving. So he did. "Thank you."

She wound his arms around his waist and hugged her body around his. "Thank *you*."

So much for keeping secrets hidden from her.

"You are one stubborn woman. You can't just say

you're welcome?" Her breath shuddered against his chest and he realized she was crying. Gut check. Embarrassing himself didn't matter. "Hey." He leaned back against her arms so he could see the redness rimming those moonlit eyes. He slicked her hair off her face and tucked it behind her ears, catching each tear that ran onto her cheek with his thumbs and stroking it away. "I never expected to see tears on you. Twice in one day now? They kind of freaked me out this afternoon. I thought you were crashing on me."

She blinked several times to stop the flow and gave a good sniffle before resting her cheek against the pad of his shoulder.

"What's going through that jumbled-up head of yours?"

"I've been thinking how, even though you mean well, you can't really stay with me until all this is settled. You'll have to go to work, and I will, too, eventually."

Her fingers wandering lazily up and down his spine weren't helping him quell the desire thrumming through his blood.

"I don't know how I would have gotten through this weekend without you. And when tomorrow comes, I think I'm really going to miss you."

"The thought of this guy getting to you again makes me crazy," he admitted. He didn't want her to be afraid for her safety. "If I can't physically be with you, I'll make sure someone I trust is. My partner, Hud, will help. Or my brothers or sister. Even Dad. He's the smartest cop I ever knew. He's still got the goods to keep an eye on you."

"No. I mean, I'm going to miss *you*." When she pulled back, the tears were gone. But there was still a hint of sadness in her eyes. "There are a lot of differences between us, Detective. I'm an older woman. Money—I know guys can be funny if a woman earns more than he does. You come from a big family and I have empty rooms. The different sides of the courtroom we each represent."

"Look, I was an idiot for holding that against you. You were doing your job, just like I was doing mine. You might still be the Terminator, but I say it with nothing but respect now."

"I know that." Those mesmerizing fingers moved to the placket of his shirt and started tracing lines up and down his chest. "But we've only known each other for what—three days? Besides this investigation, what reason do you really have to be with me?"

"This." His body couldn't take it anymore. Didn't she understand what she was doing to him? He caught her face between his hands and claimed her mouth in a hungry kiss. Her lips parted and he took full advantage of the wanton heat inside, inviting her tongue to dance with his, nipping at her bottom lip, then soothing the pliant curve with the stroke of his tongue. Her lips chased after his when he finally pulled away. He felt the pulse in her throat thumping beneath his fingertips, and her breath came in stuttered gasps that brushed the sweet pearls of her breasts against his own heaving chest.

"This *thing* happening between us doesn't have anything to do with the investigation. I don't need three days or three weeks or three years to know how much I want to be with you. I don't understand it. And maybe it's not the smartest move I've ever made with a woman. But you and I… There's something here I want to explore. Maybe physically, you're not up for much more yet, but…" The woman was smiling. Keir's fingers tunneled into her hair, but maybe he should be backing off. "What? What are you thinking?"

"That even if three days is all I ever have—I've been lucky to spend them with you."

"One. You are having a nice, long life, Counselor. Two. I'm glad I spent them with you, too. And—"

"Three." She backed him up against one of the bedposts and kissed him.

Then things got real. Fast. Kenna unbuttoned his shirt and pushed it off his shoulders. He caught the hem of her shirt and swept it off over her head. When they were chest to chest, skin to skin, he reversed positions and pinned her against the bedpost. He only abandoned her mouth to bend down to worship her breasts. He loved the tight little buds and drew them into his mouth, loving the gasps and throaty moans each touch elicited. Then Keir went down on his knees, pulling her knit bottoms down inch by inch, introducing his lips to each new stretch of soft, taut skin until he felt the goose bumps beading beneath every grasp of his hand. He tasted the crease between each hip and thigh, teased the blond thatch in between. Finally, her pants were on the floor and he was feasting his way down every quivering, incredible inch of those long, glorious legs.

"Keir… Keir…" Her fingers clutched at his hair with needy abandon. "I don't think I can stand any more."

"Patience, baby, patience." He kissed the dimple beside her knee and started to work his way back up. "I want this to be good for both of us."

The fingers in his hair were more urgent now. She was shaking. "No. Standing. I can't…"

Ah, hell. Keir pushed to his feet and picked her up. He set her on the bed, fighting to calm his deep, ragged breaths and ignore the arousal straining painfully against his zipper. Worry and a cold shower would soon put things into proper perspective again. "I'm sorry, baby." He folded the bedspread over her naked body and lay down beside her, gathering Kenna and the bulky cover into his arms. "You haven't been out of the hospital very long. Does anything hurt? You should have told me you weren't up for this. We'll stop."

"It only hurts that you're thinking about stopping." She pushed at the cover, pushed at his arms. He didn't fight when she pushed him onto his back and straddled his hips. "I meant my knees were about to buckle from what you were doing to me, and I didn't want to embarrass myself and wind up flat on the floor, and then you'd worry if I was hurt and you'd stop, and I—"

Keir sat up, catching her bottom and keeping her squarely in his lap when she would have tumbled. "You're sure? Because I want this."

Her fingers dropped to the snap of his jeans. "Me, too."

Keir pulled his wallet from his back pocket before his jeans and shorts wound up on the floor and his gun ended up on the bedside table. He bit his lip as Kenna rolled the condom over his manhood. And when he couldn't stand another bold touch, he moved on top of her, marveling at the utter perfection of how their bodies fit together. "You are the only thing on my to-do list tonight."

He stopped up her answering laugh with a kiss and pushed inside her. There were no more words, no more teasing. She wrapped those long, glorious legs around him and they rocked together in a decadent rhythm until she cried out his name and arched against him. Keir groaned with the power of his own release before falling down onto the bed beside her. He reached down to find her hand and laced their fingers together.

Yeah. Perfection.

Chapter Ten

Kenna woke with a delicious ache that had nothing to do with her injuries and everything to do with the two rounds of bliss she'd shared with the naked man sprawled out asleep in her bed with little more than a sheet draped over his hips.

She wasn't sure if the noise of the storm had waked her, or if the wishes that flitted through her dreams had demanded she make some conscious decisions about her life. Keir Watson was as kind and considerate as he was skilled and passionate. He made her think, made her laugh, made her feel cherished and safe. So she'd gotten up to visit the bathroom, then slipped back into her pajamas and curled up with a blanket in the window seat to watch the storm illuminate the night with pulses of lightning and the rain streak and chill the glass.

Kenna wasn't precisely sure what kind of life she'd lived before the attack. But the glimpses she'd seen of fear and control and loneliness didn't seem like the kind of life she wanted to live anymore. She wanted nights like this. She wanted to defend good people and help them find the justice they deserved. She wanted happiness.

She wanted love.

A bolt of lightning forked down to the earth and the answering thunder rumbled in waves for several seconds after.

"Should I be worried?"

Kenna turned to the hushed seduction of Keir's voice and smiled. He sat on the edge of the bed and smiled back before pulling on his shorts and jeans. He picked his shirt up off the floor and shrugged it over his broad shoulders as he crossed the room. She tilted her face to his and he leaned down to give her a kiss.

"Just thinking some deep thoughts."

He sat down beside her, resting his hand with a casual possession on her thigh. "Okay, now I am worried. Want to share?"

Lightning flashed.

"I was thinking about something you said this afternoon—about being successful at whatever I wanted—"

The answering explosion of thunder rattled the window, startling her.

A second later, all the yard lights went out.

Keir leaped to his feet. "The storm didn't do that."

With the pitch-darkness outside, he hurried to the bed to turn on the lamp. Nothing. "Electricity's out."

Mother Nature lit up the earth with a trio of lightning bursts, filling her backyard with fleeting moments of daylight. In the third flash, she saw him. Standing among the trees, his faceless mask angled up toward her window. "Keir!"

Kenna scrambled off the window seat as Hoodie Guy vanished into the darkness.

She ran to Keir's side as he hung up the bedside phone.

"He's cut the landline, too." He tucked his gun into the waistband of his jeans, snatched up the spare keys to the house and pushed his cell phone into her hands before running out the door.

Kenna dropped the blanket and hurried down the stairs behind him.

"Call 9-1-1. Give them my name and this address and tell Dispatch that an officer needs assistance."

He punched in the security code and threw open the front door. Kenna grabbed his arm, trying to stop him. "You're going out there?"

But he was already slipping out of her grip. "He's not coming in here. Lock up behind me. I've got my own key. Don't let anyone else in."

"Keir?"

He charged down the steps and circled the house to catch the intruder by surprise. She caught a glimpse of his white shirt near the garage at the next flash of lightning. And then he was gone. Swallowed up by the rain and darkness. Kenna locked the door and felt her way through the dining room to the kitchen. She called 9-1-1 and remained on the line as the dispatcher asked. Then she pulled a butcher knife from the drawer beside the stove and crouched down behind the island, praying that Keir would be the one to find her.

"AH, HELL." KEIR SAW the truck parked on the far side of the garage and finally knew the answer.

He swiped the rain from his face and darted through the dark garage. Muddy work boots. The same kind of boots that had left the tracks at the parking garage. Free passkey onto the estate anytime he wanted. Hoodie Guy didn't need to get into the house when the boss lady came out to talk to him every time he worked in the yard. Keir still didn't know the why. But Marvin Bennett was done terrorizing Kenna.

He wished he could risk using a flashlight to follow the muddy tracks over the flagstones into the trees in the backyard before the rain washed them away. But he couldn't risk giving away his position to a man who was more familiar with these surroundings than Keir was.

The gardener hadn't been covering up Kenna's gardening mistake that day they found him rebuilding the brick wall. He'd been covering up his own crime scene. Painting over Kenna's blood where she'd either fallen or been shoved against the bricks. He'd probably tried to burn some other kind of evidence in the fire pit, like rosebushes that had been crushed or broken in a struggle. Bennett was a damn cool customer, being surprised by a cop and the woman he was obsessed with—the woman he thought he'd killed—and going on like some kind of idiot who barely knew his way around a flowerpot. He'd kept his wits about him the night before, too, moving Kenna's body to that downtown alley. When Keir first saw Bennett in disguise, he'd probably been watching the alley to see if anyone discovered her body.

Had Kenna figured out who'd been sending her rose petals and making those disturbing calls? Had she made an accusation? Caught him doing something suspicious? Had she simply given the gardener one order too many and he'd snapped?

Whether the murder attempt itself was planned or accidental, stalking Kenna for weeks leading up to the attack—seeing her often enough that he could watch and enjoy his handiwork as she grew angry and paranoid, helpless and afraid—meant Bennett had a game plan here. It might have started as a quest for vengeance or a sick obsession. But Bennett was here tonight to end the game. He'd already gotten one taste of Kenna's blood. And clearly, he was here for more.

Keir stopped beside the shelter of a giant locust tree. He silenced his breathing, listening for any sounds of movement in the noisy storm. He wondered if Kenna had placed the call for backup and how long it would take other cops to get here. She might not have that kind of time. He needed to confront Bennett and take him out himself.

Just as Keir opened his mouth to shout Bennett's name, lightning flashed in the sky overhead, silhouetting branches and leaves and the shovel swinging at his head. Keir tried to dodge the blow. The shovel glanced off his temple but smacked his head into the tree's unyielding trunk. Pain jolted through his skull. Lightning danced across his vision and he crumpled to the ground.

Keir's last thoughts were of Marvin Bennett rifling through Keir's pockets for his keys, picking up his gun and running toward the house, and the knowledge he hadn't told Kenna he loved her.

KENNA WAS SHAKING so badly that she'd been forced to set the cell phone on the floor beside her so she wouldn't drop it and make a noise that would give her hiding place away. Instead, she clung to the handle of the knife with both hands and prayed she'd never have to use it.

When she heard the key turning in the lock of the patio door, the breath she'd been holding rushed out in a noisy huff and she set the knife on top of the island and pulled herself to her feet. But the man in the black hoodie was locking the door behind him. The faceless mask was pure terror as he crossed the long room, and Kenna was suddenly as cold as the marble countertop.

"Hello, Kenna," he rasped in that toneless voice. Lightning fluttered like a strobe light behind him, silhouetting his familiar shape and giving her a glimpse of the gun he pointed at her. It was Keir's weapon. "I'm afraid Lover Boy isn't here to rescue you anymore."

"What have you done to him?"

She lunged for the knife, but he fired off a wide shot that hit the cabinet behind her and she froze, raising her hands. "Now, be a good girl and toss that knife over here."

After she did what he said, he unzipped his jacket and shoved the hood off his head. He slipped the butcher knife through his belt next to the long sheath with the knife he'd used against her earlier. Shrinking back against the opposite counter, she felt her foot come down on Keir's phone and she wondered if the dispatcher could hear what was happening and rush an ambulance and the entire police force here before she and Keir died.

When he pulled off the ski mask, Kenna gasped and collapsed against the counter. "Oh, my God." How long had this creep been right under her nose? How many conversations had they shared? How many times had she patted him on the back or shaken his hand? *He doesn't get to win.* Tears burned her eyes as she thought of Keir lying wounded or dead outside. She pulled herself up straight and articulated the name for the woman listening in. "Marvin Bennett."

She nudged the phone under the lip of the cabinet as he reached the island and circled toward her. "It's just you and me and the task I wanted to finish last night. I've enjoyed seeing you afraid. Watching how you tried to control your fear by controlling everything else in your life. I wanted you to suffer the way she did."

"The way who did?"

"Genie. My daughter."

Kenna backed toward the dining room door, wondering if she could get through it before he fired off another shot. "I didn't know you had a daughter."

"She killed herself six years ago. Two years after she'd been raped."

"Raped?" Kenna halted. This was about Brian Elliott.

"The Rose Red Rapist. Your biggest case. You made headlines—and a fortune defending that scum who ruined my daughter's life."

"Genie D'Angelo." She remembered the name from the case file she'd read. "Genie is your daughter?"

"Was. That's an important distinction, Kenna. You're the one who likes to get every detail right."

"I'm so sorry, Marvin. I didn't know."

"Move away from that door." He pointed the gun at her and gestured for her to walk toward the sectional sofa. When she didn't immediately respond, he snagged her by the elbow and dragged her there. "D'Angelo was her married name. But her marriage couldn't survive what that bastard Elliott had done to her. She wouldn't let her husband touch her. She barely let me—her own father—comfort her. Every day was a misery for her after the rape. She went into a depression. She slashed her wrists once. I found her and got her to the hospital. But I didn't know about the pills. I couldn't save her from the pills."

"You blame me for her death."

"No." He threw her onto the couch and she tried to scramble away, but he caught her by the ankle and dragged her back to press his knee into her gut and lean over her. He drew the tip of the gun across the stitches on her jaw. "I blame you for Brian Elliott still being alive."

Kenna could barely catch her breath to speak. "I was just doing my job. I never condoned anything he did. Every person in this country deserves a fair trial—"

He back-handed her across the face and she felt the cut on her cheek split open.

"You defended him! You kept him from the lethal injection he deserved."

"Rape isn't a capital offense. But he's probably going to die in prison before he's ever released—"

"Shut up! He shouldn't be living any kind of life. And it's all your fault." He dipped his gloved fingers in the blood on her cheek and drew an X over her heart. "I wanted you to suffer the way Genie did. Elliott violated her in so many ways, and then had the gall to leave a rose on her beaten body? She hated roses after that. I'm a gardener. I raise beautiful flowers. But she couldn't even look at them."

"So you sent me roses." Her fingers clenched in the sofa cushions, seeking a weapon to defend herself from the man who surely intended to kill her.

"I wanted to cut you—the way she cut herself."

Cut. The answer was staring her right in the face. Yes, a gun was being pointed to her heart, but her hands were free and that butcher knife was within her reach.

"When you came to me on Friday and said you wanted me to rip out all the rosebushes and plant hydrangeas, I lost my temper. They're supposed to be there to remind you of my daughter. They're supposed to remind you of that horrible man you defended. The roses were there to haunt you and make you suffer the way my little girl did. So I pulled my knife out to stop you. We fought. And when I cracked your head open and saw all that blood, I thought I'd killed you." His face twisted up as if he was about to cry. "You ruined everything. You weren't supposed to die until last night. I had to get you out of here and reset the stage for your death. But then that stupid cop was here, and I couldn't. But I've taken care of him. He won't stop me now."

Keir. Kenna's heart squeezed in her chest. What had this lunatic done to him? Kenna wanted to make sure there would be justice for the man she loved. She wanted the dispatcher to hear everything. "Why last night? What was so important about your deadline?"

"Because of Genie. This is all for my daughter. This is justice. I wanted you to know just how many days you had left to live. I wanted you to die on the same date my Genie did."

"I didn't know it was you, Marvin. I couldn't remember your face or what happened. I still don't. You could have walked away a free man."

"Forgetting's not good enough. My Genie could never forget her suffering." He pressed the gun into her breast, pinning her as he unhooked the sheath on his belt. "That's no better than Elliott's punishment. You don't get to forget, either."

Another flash of lightning lit up the night sky, giving her a glimpse of Keir Watson at her patio door, swinging a shovel at the wall of glass.

Thunder shook the house as the panes of glass splintered and crashed. Marvin raised the gun and Kenna reached for the knife on his belt.

"Bennett!" Keir shouted.

The blast of the gunshot deafened her ears and the ejected casing hit her arm, singeing her skin.

Her fingers fell short of snatching the blade and she heard the feral roar of Keir charging across the room.

"Let her go!"

Instead of obeying Keir's order, Marvin hauled her up off the couch and pulled her in front of him to use as a shield. She saw the blood staining the shoulder of Keir's mud-stained shirt and would have cried out. But Marvin squeezed his forearm around her throat and ground the gun barrel into her temple.

Keir halted a few feet away and dropped the shovel he carried and raised his hands to placate her abductor. "No one has to die here, Bennett."

"She does." Kenna fingered the knife butting against her hip but couldn't get it to budge. "I want you to watch her die, too."

"I'm not going to let you do it."

"Better idea." Marvin pointed the gun toward Keir. "I'll kill you first. That'll make her suffer more."

"No!" Kenna got a grip of the knife and yanked it from Marvin's belt, slicing a cut across his shirt and belly as she pulled it out.

Marvin cursed as he pulled the trigger, firing a wild shot. Startled by pain, he loosened his hold on her.

"Get down!" Keir yelled, charging toward Marvin. Kenna dove for the floor as Keir sailed over the couch and tackled Marvin. The gun flew from his hand and got knocked beneath the coffee table. The two men fought, grunting and cursing. Marvin punched at Keir's wound and Keir lost his grip on Marvin's neck.

"Look out!" Kenna warned when she saw Marvin's fingers find the gun and close around it. "Gun!"

Marvin turned the gun on Keir. But Keir had armed himself, too.

Before Marvin could fire, Keir rammed the knife straight into the old man's heart.

MARVIN'S HAND DROPPED to the floor and Keir pried his gun from the dead man's grasp. He stood up slowly, hearing the wail of sirens through the noise of the storm.

His shoulder was throbbing where he'd been shot, he had a rotten headache and he'd cut his left heel on the broken glass near the door. But nothing was going to stop him from catching Kenna when she ran to him and wound her arms around his neck. "Keir. Oh, Keir. I thought…I thought he'd killed you."

He wanted to stab Bennett again when he saw the blood oozing down her cheek and marking her shirt. "You okay, baby?"

"I'm fine."

That was all he needed to hear. He slipped his good arm around her waist and walked her away from the dead body. They ended up in the darkened foyer, where he opened the front door. Then he sat on the stairs where the approaching police would see him and pulled Kenna into his lap.

"You've been shot. And what's this scrape on your head? I can't believe it's finally over. How am I ever going to repay you?"

He set his gun on the step beside him and tunneled his fingers into her beautiful hair. "Just listen to me for a minute without interrupting. I need to say this. You need to know this right now, before all those other cops come pouring in here, before we make our statements, before we get whisked away in an ambulance to the hospital. Will you do that?"

He could tell it was killing her to keep her mouth shut, but she nodded.

"I love you, Kenna Parker. It may not make any sense for it to happen this fast or for two people who are so different to make a relationship work." She opened her mouth to argue, but he pressed his thumb against her lips. "You promised."

She clamped her mouth shut.

"I've done this all backward with you. I was carrying you in my arms before we were even properly introduced. I want to kiss you every day of my life and argue with you and make love to you and laugh with you—and I don't even know when your birthday is or what your favorite color might be. I want to ask you out on a date and get to know you and see if the age and money make any kind of difference. But I know they won't. Because we belong together. And I hope that when we get out in the real world and get a regular night's sleep and crazy men aren't out to hurt you… You may never remember the night of your attack, but I will never forget the seventy-two hours that followed."

He'd run out of words. But he hoped he'd said enough. He couldn't have risked waiting a moment longer to spill his heart.

When he pulled his thumb away, she smiled. "Do I get to talk now?"

He nodded.

"I love you, too. I love the idea of kissing you every day and arguing with you—hopefully, not too often. I want to make love to you and laugh with you. My birthday is March tenth, my favorite color is the blue of your beautiful eyes and if you ever want to ask me out on a date, I'll say yes. But…"

Keir was grinning all the way down to his heart. "You're arguing already?"

"You don't think this time we've spent together qualifies as a first date? We haven't been separated since I stumbled out of that alley. If you take away the stalker and the amnesia, the rest of it was a lot of special. I loved spending that time with you."

"Then we finally agree about something." He slipped his arm around her and, cautious of each other's injuries, leaned in for a kiss. "Best. Date. Ever."

Epilogue

The unhappy man opened the newspaper to the page where the ink was smeared because he'd looked at the picture and read the announcement so many times before. He handed it across the desk to the younger man sitting in the leather chair drinking a glass of *his* finest gin. "Niall Watson's engagement announcement. They're planning a fall wedding."

The other man set down the glass and picked up the paper to read the details. "Well, ain't that sweet? They're gettin' married on the old man's birthday."

"It isn't sweet, and it isn't acceptable." The unhappy man pulled a gun and silencer from the top drawer of his desk while the man he'd hired amused himself by reading the announcement out loud.

"Oh, that's rich. They're even going to do it at the same church."

"Yes. I'm sure it's some kind of testament to the Watson family's will to survive and succeed despite the tragedy of Olivia's wedding."

The other man set down the newspaper, picking up on the disgust in his tone. "You said you didn't want dead bodies—that a clean kill was too good for them—even though I said it was a mistake. You wanted chaos and suffering. I did what you paid me to do."

"That's not good enough. Not anymore." His blood was boiling with rage at the injustice of it all. They'd forgotten her. Thomas Watson had stolen Mary from him and she'd been murdered and forgotten. But stroking the trigger of the gun beneath the desk was the only outward expression of his roiling emotions. "Shooting the old man was supposed to destroy them. But they're going on with their lives as if nothing happened. They're happier than ever."

"I can finish the old man if you want. In his condition, it wouldn't be hard."

"You had your chance." The unhappy man raised the weapon and shot his guest twice in the chest. He set down the gun and pulled a pocketknife from his trousers as he walked around the desk. He tipped the slumped man back in his chair and cut the fancy buckle off his belt. He fingered the notches carved into the silver, then slid the buckle into his own pocket, along with the knife. "This will be the trophy for *my* kill."

He picked up the glass and finished off the drink in one long swallow. Then he returned to his seat and placed a phone call. "I have a situation I need you to clean up for me. I'll pay your usual fee." He started to hang up but put the phone back to his ear. "Do you have anyone inside KCPD you can trust?"

"Does this have anything to do with the situation I'm cleaning up?"

"No. I need some information."

"I know someone who owes me a favor."

"Good. I want to meet with him tomorrow."

* * * * *

*Look for the next thrilling installment
in* USA TODAY *bestselling author
Julie Miller's suspenseful miniseries*
THE PRECINCT: BACHELORS IN BLUE,
coming in 2017!

*Look for it wherever
Harlequin Intrigue books are sold.*

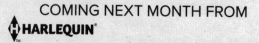

SPECIAL EXCERPT FROM

MIRA®

A popular girl goes missing, and everyone close to her has something to hide.

*Go inside the mind of a criminal in the fourth book in the riveting **THE PROFILER** series: STALKED by Elizabeth Heiter.*

"Where are you, Haley?" Linda whispered into the stillness of her daughter's room.

Today marked exactly a month since her daughter had gone missing. Since Haley's boyfriend, Jordan, had dropped her off at school for cheerleading practice. Since her best friend Marissa had waved to her from the field on that unusually warm day, watched her walk into the school, presumably to change before joining Marissa at practice.

She'd never walked out again.

How did a teenage girl go missing from *inside* her high school? No one could answer that for Linda. As time went by, they seemed to have fewer answers and more questions.

But Linda *knew*—with some deep part of her she could only explain as mother's intuition—that Haley was out there somewhere. Not buried in an unmarked grave, as she'd overheard two cops speculating when day after day passed with no more clues. Haley was still alive, and just waiting for someone to bring her home.

Linda clutched Haley's bright pink sweatshirt tighter. She fell against the bed, trying to hold her sobs in, and the mattress slid away from her, away from the box spring.

Linda froze as the edge of a tiny black notebook caught her attention.

The book was jammed between the box spring and the bed frame. The police must have missed it, because she'd seen them peer underneath Haley's mattress when they'd looked through the room, assessing her daughter's things so matter-of-factly.

Linda's pulse skyrocketed as she yanked it out. She didn't recognize the notebook, but when she opened the cover, there was no mistaking her daughter's girlie handwriting. And the words…

She dropped the notebook, practically flung it away from her in her desire to get rid of it, to unsee it. She didn't realize she'd started screaming until her husband ran into the room and wrapped his arms around her.

"What? What is it?" he kept asking, but all she could do was sob and point a shaking hand at the notebook, lying open to the first page, and Haley's distinctive scrawl:

If you're reading this, I'm already dead.

Follow FBI profiler Evelyn Baine as she tries to uncover which of Haley's secrets might have led to her disappearance.

STALKED
by Elizabeth Heiter
Available December 27, 2016,
from MIRA Books.

$1.00 OFF

ELIZABETH HEITER

Secrets can be deadly...

MIRA®

Available December 27, 2016

Order your copy today!

ELIZABETH
HEITER

USA TODAY BESTSELLING AUTHOR

STALKED

"Suspenseful from the start
and intriguing throughout.
RECOMMENDED!"
—LEE CHILD
#1 NEW YORK TIMES
BESTSELLING AUTHOR
ON *SEIZED*

$7.99 U.S./$9.99 CAN.

---✂

$1.00 OFF

the purchase price of STALKED by Elizabeth Heiter.

Offer valid from December 17, 2016, to June 17, 2017.
Redeemable at participating retail outlets, in-store only. Not redeemable at
Barnes & Noble. Limit one coupon per purchase. Valid in the U.S.A. and Canada only.

52614428

5 65373 00076 2   (8100)0 12233

® and ™ are trademarks owned and used by the trademark owner and/or its licensee.
© 2016 Harlequin Enterprises Limited

MCOUPEH1216